Something darted out from the trees.

Adam had his gun in hand in an instant, his arm pressing Charlotte down and out of the line of fire.

He knew how quickly safety could turn to danger, and he knew how desperate the Night Stalker must be. The local papers had run the story.

Guardian Angel Saves Tenth Victim of Notorious Night Stalker.

The reporters might not have Charlotte's name, but they were speculating that she was someone local to Whisper Lake.

How long would it take the Night Stalker to figure out who she was and where she lived?

Leaves rustled. A twig snapped. A dog appeared.

"Clover!" Charlotte shouted, and then she was scrambling out of the car and onto the road.

He grabbed her, hauling her up and into the SUV. Not caring about her injury. All he cared about was keeping her alive.

If the dog loping toward them was hers, someone had let it out. Someone who might be waiting for her to return, waiting for her to go looking for the dog she obviously loved. Waiting on the road with a gun in hand, ready to finish what he'd begun.

Aside from her faith and her family, there's not much **Shirlee McCoy** enjoys more than a good book! When she's not teaching or chauffeuring her five kids, she can usually be found plotting her next Love Inspired Suspense story or wandering around the beautiful Inland Northwest in search of inspiration. Shirlee loves to hear from readers. If you have time, drop her a line at shirlee@shirleemccoy.com.

Books by Shirlee McCoy

Love Inspired Suspense

Special Crimes Unit

Night Stalker

Mission: Rescue

Protective Instincts
Her Christmas Guardian
Exit Strategy
Deadly Christmas Secrets
Mystery Child
The Christmas Target
Mistaken Identity
Christmas on the Run

Classified K-9 Unit

Bodyguard

Rookie K-9 Unit

Secrets and Lies

Visit the Author Profile page
at Harlequin.com for more titles.

Night Stalker

Shirlee McCoy

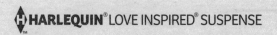

HARLEQUIN® LOVE INSPIRED® SUSPENSE

Recycling programs
for this product may
not exist in your area.

LOVE INSPIRED BOOKS

ISBN-13: 978-1-335-54361-5

Night Stalker

Copyright © 2018 by Shirlee McCoy

www.Harlequin.com

Printed in U.S.A.

When thou passest through the waters, I will be with thee; and through the rivers, they shall not overflow thee: when thou walkest through the fire, thou shalt not be burned; neither shall the flame kindle upon thee.
—*Isaiah* 43:2

To you: the reader who has followed me from Lakeview, Virginia, to Whisper Lake, Maine. May you find joy in every sunrise and peace in every circumstance, and may the fullness of His love and mercy sustain you through every heartache.

ONE

Charlotte Murray hated the lake.

She hated the blue-green water that gleamed like black ink in the moonlight, the quiet lap of waves against the shore, the whisper of damp air rustling through the tall reeds that bordered her yard. She hated it, but she couldn't make herself leave.

Six years after her four-year-old son, Daniel, had wandered outside and drowned, five and a half years after her husband, Adam, left, five years after the divorce was finalized, and here she sat, the old swing creaking as she rocked in the early-morning darkness. How many sleepless nights had she spent staring out at Whisper Lake, wondering what she could have done to change things?

Too many.

Her friends said she needed to move on. Her therapist had encouraged her to rent out the cottage, move into town and create a new life for herself. One not defined by the tragedy of losing her son. *It's time to join the living again*, he'd said as if there were some limit to grief and some timeline for recovery that she should be following.

She hadn't been back to see him since.

Grief eased. It didn't go away. Not even as time passed or environments changed.

"Besides," she murmured, "I've got a job, friends, volunteer work. It's not like I spend all of my time staring at the lake and dwelling on what I can't change."

Clover whined and dropped his boxy head on her knee, the added weight stopping the swaying motion of the swing. At seventy pounds, the poodle mix was double the size the county animal shelter had said he would be. Charlotte didn't mind. He filled up more of the house, took up a little of the extra space that had been left when Daniel died and Adam walked out.

She scratched behind Clover's floppy ears, kissed his velvety muzzle. "Ready to go inside?"

He was on his feet before she finished speaking, trotting to the back door, doing his goofy little poodle prance. She'd chosen him out of desperation, wanting something to keep the silence from smothering her. Before Daniel's death, she and Adam had talked about getting a therapy dog, one that would bond with their son and maybe enter his solitary world. They'd planned it as a Christmas surprise.

Daniel had died in the summer. She didn't remember the Christmas following his death. She only remembered the emptiness of the house after Adam packed his bags and walked out. She remembered the heaviness of the air and of her sorrow. She remembered the anger that had simmered beneath the surface of that.

She had thought their relationship was strong enough to weather anything.

But anything had not included the death of their son.

She stepped into the mudroom, old linoleum crackling beneath her feet. A wide doorway led into the 1920s-style kitchen, the farmhouse sink and yellow subway tile just quaint enough to be chic. She and Adam had painted the walls ivory and the old pine cabinets bright white. Adam's job as deputy sheriff of Whisper Lake, Maine, hadn't paid much, but they'd managed to make the cottage their home. They'd been a team back then. Daniel's autism diagnosis had tossed them into the deep water of parenting, and they'd clung to each other to keep from going under.

That had changed after Daniel's death. Somehow, rather than mourning together, they'd mourned apart, their grief a raw wound between them, a deep chasm that neither had been able to cross.

Even after so many years, Charlotte sometimes wondered if she could have changed things. A word spoken into the silence. A hug offered at just the right time. Tears shared rather than hidden. Maybe they'd still be together.

But maybe not.

Probably not.

They'd been middle school kids when they'd met. Best friends. Allies. High school sweethearts. Too young to understand how challenging and heartbreaking life could be.

Floorboards creaked as she stepped into the small living room. *Cozy* was the word her grandmother had always used. *Tiny* was a more accurate description. When Daniel died, Charlotte and Adam had been saving money to build an addition. Instead, they'd purchased a burial plot and a casket.

Charlotte frowned. It had been years since she'd thought about that. So many dreams had died with Daniel. She'd created new dreams, crafted a new life, imagined herself leaving Whisper Lake dozens of times. Stayed through summers and autumns and long winters. Into springs and back through summers again. Seasons passing—life passing—while she sat on the swing on the back porch.

Would she still be there five years from now? Ten? Twenty-five? That was the question she'd been asking herself recently. The cottage had been standing in this spot for nearly a hundred years, the Sears Roebuck bungalow built by her great-grandfather and passed down from one family member to another. Her grandmother had deeded it to her a year before Daniel's death—a twenty-first birthday gift and a celebration of the fact that Charlotte had made it through high school and college despite the challenges of teen pregnancy and a special-needs child.

Pregnant at seventeen. Married at eighteen. Grieving parent at twenty-two. Divorced at twenty-three. And now, at twenty-eight, alone and mostly happy about it. It was hard to be hurt when there was no one around to hurt you. The cottage held memories and sorrows, but being there was solitary and safe, and she craved that as much as she craved anything.

Clover loped through the living room, stopping near the front window, his head cocked to the side, his attention on the floor-length curtains. The lights were off, but she could see him there, a dark shadow in the gloom, his body stiff, his tail high and still. He growled, the sound making the hair on the back of her neck stand on end.

Clover didn't growl.

He rarely barked.

His happy-go-lucky, calm personality made him the perfect therapy dog.

"What's wrong, boy?" she asked, creeping to the window and easing the curtains back.

It was still dark, the first rays of sun hours away. The motion-sensor porch lights hadn't been tripped, and the yard looked empty, the old maple tree a hulking shadow against the blue-black sky.

Clover growled again, pressing his nose against the windowpane.

Beyond the yard, a narrow dirt road separated her property from state land. Out here, there were more animals than people, more trees than houses and more hiking trails than roads. The only other house on Charlotte's street belonged to Bubbles, her elderly neighbor. The octogenarian wandered the lake shore and the woods at all times of the day and night, collecting leaves and flowers, mushrooms and wild herbs. Charlotte had cautioned her to be careful. She wasn't as young as she used to be, and it was very easy to get lost and hurt in the Maine wilderness. People died there. People disappeared. But Bubbles had grown up on the lake. She'd learned the land before she'd learned to read.

At least, that was what she'd told Charlotte.

Still, Charlotte worried, and Clover's behavior made her worry more.

"Stay," Charlotte commanded as she walked to the front door and opened it. Clover whined but dropped down onto his belly.

Good. The last thing she wanted was her dog getting in a tussle with a bear or a bobcat. More than likely, that was what he'd been growling at. On the off chance that Bubbles was outside, hurt or in trouble, Charlotte would take a quick walk to her property and make certain the old house was locked up tight. She grabbed her cell phone and tucked it into her pocket but didn't bother grabbing the bowie knife she carried when she hiked. Whatever had been outside was probably long gone by now.

She stepped onto the porch, the security light turning on immediately. Somewhere in the distance an engine was rumbling. Surprised, Charlotte stood still and listened. The nearest paved road was a quarter mile away and stretched from the small town of Whisper Lake to its closest neighbor twenty miles away. During the day, the road got some traffic, but at night it was usually quiet.

A soft cry drifted through the darkness.

An animal?

She told herself it was, but her heart was racing, her pulse thrumming. Winter-dry grass snapped beneath her feet, the cold spring air seeping through her jeans and sweater. She reached the old fence that marked the beginning of Bubble's property and stepped onto the road to get around it. A few hundred yards away, the house jutted up from the grassy landscape. Victorian and ornate, it had been on the bluff overlooking Whisper Lake for more than a century. Bubble's family had owned it for most of that time.

It didn't take long to reach the driveway. Bubble's Oldsmobile was parked there, its glossy paint gleaming. The house was quiet, curtains pulled across the windows, the lights off. Charlotte tried the front door. Locked. Just like she'd hoped. The back door was locked, too.

Everything looked just as it should, but the air crackled with electricity and the engine still hummed in the distance. She went back to the road, told herself that she should go home, but something made her turn left instead of right. Toward the crossroad. Away from the cottage. Heading toward the stop sign and the paved road beyond it. She'd just reached it when something crashed through the trees a dozen yards away.

She jumped, her hand reaching for the bowie knife she hadn't bothered bringing. A stupid mistake. One she vowed to never make again. There were predators out here. Usually, they didn't bother people. Sometimes, though, food was scarce, they were hungry and they went after anything weaker than them.

Just head, asphalt marked the end of the private road she lived on. Headlights illuminated the dark pavement and a purse that lay abandoned there. Its contents had spilled out. Wallet. Lipstick. Keys. Phone. A few other odds and ends. None of them belonged in the middle of a country road in the darkest hours of the morning.

She pulled out her cell phone and dialed 911, staying out of the vehicle's headlights. A truck. She could see that. Passenger door open. She couldn't see the driver's door.

That made her nervous.

The entire situation made her nervous.

She took a step back, the 911 operator's voice ringing hollowly in her ear.

"Nine-one-one. What's the nature of your emergency?"

"I need the police," Charlotte responded, her focus on the truck, the open door, the purse.

"What—"

A woman screamed, the sound breaking the early-morning quiet and masking whatever else the operator said.

Charlotte whirled toward the sound, scanning the trees and the darkness, her heart pounding so frantically, she thought it might fly from her chest.

"Ma'am? Are you still there?" the 911 operator asked.

"I need the police," she repeated, rattling off the address.

She could hear the heavy pant of someone's breath, the thud of feet on dead leaves. A man stepped onto the road, his back to Charlotte, his body oddly misshapen.

She almost called out to him, but something kept her silent. A warning of danger that she heeded.

"Ma'am? Can you tell me what's happening? Are you in danger?" the 911 operator asked.

As if he'd heard the words, the man swung around.

She realized the truth about two seconds too late.

He wasn't misshapen.

He was carrying someone—a woman slung over his shoulders in a fireman's carry.

Charlotte could think of a lot of reasons he might be doing that. Most of them weren't good. Kidnapping came to mind. Carjacking. Murder.

Her instincts were telling her to run, but her conscience insisted she stay.

"What's going on?" she called out, and the man took a step in her direction. Seemed to change his mind and turned toward the truck again.

The 911 operator was speaking, but Charlotte couldn't make sense of the words. She was focused on the man. The open truck door. The escape that would be at hand once he got his victim into the vehicle.

"Put her down," she demanded, and he swung around again.

He didn't speak.

He didn't warn her.

One minute, he was holding the woman. The next, he dropped her like she was a bag of garbage he'd brought to the dump.

"If you leave—" Charlotte began, planning to tell him that he could escape before the police arrived, that he could disappear and never be found.

But he moved quickly, his body silhouetted

by headlights, his face hidden as he lifted his arm, pointed at her.

The world exploded, and she was flying, landing in soft grass and scratchy pine needles, her breath gone, the world spinning. Sky. Trees. Ground. Lake. The man. Moving toward her, a dark blur spinning like everything else.

She should be scared. She knew that, but her thoughts were sluggish, her limbs leaden. She couldn't run if she wanted to. Couldn't get up.

She heard sirens, feet on pavement, an engine roaring to life. Felt blood oozing from her chest, blood slushing in her ears.

Someone knelt beside her. Not the man. A woman. Hair in her face, hands pressing against the wound in Charlotte's chest.

"Don't die," the woman murmured.

She said something else, but the words were drowned out by the starless sky, the cool spring morning, the screaming sirens and the velvety darkness that swallowed them all.

Charlotte had changed.

That shouldn't have surprised Special Agent Adam Whitfield. He hadn't seen his ex-wife in five years. A lot had happened since then. He'd completed his master's in criminal profiling and had joined the FBI. He'd rented an apartment in the suburbs of Boston, created an entirely new life for himself.

He was nothing like the twenty-four-year-old kid who'd driven away from Whisper Lake. He shouldn't have expected that Charlotte would be the same person he'd left behind. He hadn't expected it.

But he'd still been shocked when he'd seen her. Not because she was connected to machines, tubes running from her chest and her arms. He'd been prepared for that. He hadn't been prepared to see how thin she'd become, how frail. Her cheekbones were chiseled, her jawline defined. Even her hands were thinner, her fingers longer and leaner.

In the seventy-two hours since he'd arrived, he'd gotten used to the tubes, to the hushed whisper of her breathing and the soft hiss of oxygen. He hadn't gotten used to the newer, frailer version of his ex-wife.

The woman he'd been friends with, fallen in love with, married.

The one he'd had a son with.

Lost a son with.

Abandoned.

He frowned.

Abandoned was a harsh word, but an accurate one. He'd walked out on Charlotte because he hadn't been able to bear walking past Daniel's empty bedroom every morning. He'd wanted a fresh start in a new place, and he'd thought that Charlotte would want the same. When she'd refused to move away with him, he'd left the cottage, the town and the lake with his head high and his heart shattered.

He hadn't looked back, hadn't returned for even a visit. Hadn't called to see how she was, hadn't checked in on her to see if she needed anything. They'd split their marital assets, washed their hands of one another and moved on.

Or that was what they were supposed to have done.

Moving on from the person who held your heart wasn't easy.

Now he was there, noticing the deep hollows beneath Charlotte's cheekbones and the dark circles beneath her eyes. She'd cut her hair short and lost too much weight, but if he let himself, he knew he could still see the girl she'd been when she'd walked into his seventh-grade classroom all those years ago.

He brushed a strand of straight black hair from her cheek.

"Are you in there, Charlotte?" he asked.

She didn't respond. Not with a twitch or a flutter of her eyelids. If they'd still been married, he'd have touched her cheek, lifted her limp hand and squeezed it gently. He'd have leaned close and whispered that he was there and that everything was going to be okay.

Instead, he let his hand drop away, settled back into his chair. He was tired, his muscles stiff from too many hours sitting. When he wasn't working, he liked to keep active—running, hiking, rock climbing, kayaking. Being still and quiet wasn't his thing and never had been.

"You should go for a walk," his boss, Wren Santino, said, breaking the silence.

"You've made that suggestion a dozen times in the past couple of hours," he responded, meeting her dark eyes.

"And?"

"I haven't done it yet."

"If you had, I wouldn't have to keep suggesting it," she replied reasonably.

"I want to be here when she wakes up."

"Because you're hoping to question her?" It was a legitimate question. Adam had planned to travel to Whisper Lake after he'd received a call from the Maine State Police saying that they might have another victim of the Night Stalker. One that had survived.

At the time, he'd had no idea that Charlotte was involved. All he'd known was that a young nurse had been abducted from the Whisper Lake Medical Center, that she'd escaped thanks to a Good Samaritan who'd been shot while intervening. That she fit the profile of the victims of a serial killer Adam and the FBI's Special Crimes Unit had been pursuing for years. The Maine State Police thought it was possible—even probable—that her abductor was the Night Stalker.

Adam had been ready to travel to Whisper Lake to speak with the local police, interview the nurse and decide for himself whether the case fit the Night Stalker's MO. He'd shoved aside thoughts of Daniel and Charlotte. He'd reminded himself that he had a job to do. He'd already had his vehicle packed for the trip when Wren had called him into her office and shown him the case file she'd received from the state PD. That was when he'd seen Charlotte's name. That was when he'd understood just how personal the Night Stalker case had become.

It was also when Wren had informed him that he wouldn't be part of the FBI team traveling to Maine. She planned to keep him in the loop but felt that it would be better for him and for Charlotte if he kept his distance.

He'd argued.

She'd insisted, so he'd taken personal leave and headed to Whisper Lake against her wishes.

Because he couldn't not be there.

It didn't matter that he and Charlotte were divorced. It didn't matter that they hadn't seen each other for five years. He wouldn't let her lie in a hospital bed without family to advocate for her. He'd known that with her grandparents gone, she'd have no one.

Now she had him.

"I take it you're not going to answer?" Wren said, taking a sip from a carryout cup of coffee.

"She may have seen his face," he responded, sidestepping the question.

"I suppose this would be a good time to remind you that you're on leave."

"You've reminded me every hour on the hour since we arrived."

"That's an exaggeration," she said with a half smile.

"Not much of one."

"You know this guy's MO better than anyone. You should be lead on this case," she responded. No judgment. Just a statement of the facts as she saw them.

"Charlotte has no family. She needs someone in her corner."

"She has our team. We're not going to let

anything happen to her. And not just because she's a possible witness."

"She needs someone she's familiar with. Someone who knows her."

"I could argue that she has people she's familiar with and who know her. This is a small town. If we let news of her injury leak out, she'll have plenty of friends standing in her corner."

"If her identity leaks out—" he began.

"You don't have to explain, Adam. We're all aware of how dangerous that could be."

Law enforcement had kept Charlotte's identity quiet. Aside from her neighbor, Bubbles, only medical personnel knew she was the person who'd intervened in the attempted abduction. The less information available to the public, the less information available to the Night Stalker and the easier it would be to ensure Charlotte's safety.

"Just so you know," he said, "I'm not planning to leave Whisper Lake until she's recovered enough to know what's going on and what her options are."

"Which options are we talking about? Because the way I see things, the only option she has is to cooperate with the investigation."

"You gave Bethany Andrews the choice of staying in town with police protection or going into witness protection until the Night Stalker is apprehended." The young nurse had chosen to enter witness protection. She'd been terrified that the man who'd abducted her after her shift at Whisper Lake Medical Center would come after her again.

"She and her fiancé are entering the program together. Currently, Bethany is in a secure location while she waits for medical clearance to travel. She did sustain a concussion and some memory loss from the attack. Charlotte's situation is different."

"How so?"

"She was never the Night Stalker's intended victim."

"She was the person who stopped him from getting what he wanted," he pointed out.

Wren nodded her agreement. "True, and if she saw the shooter, we may be able to close this case quickly."

"Quickly? We've put a lot of time and manpower into stopping the Night Stalker." Five years. Four states. Nine victims. All emergency room nurses who had been abducted after late-night shifts. All killed by single gunshot wounds to their heads, their bodies discovered weeks to months after they'd disappeared. Ballistic testing had proved that the weapon used had been the same with each victim. A savvy Boston police detective had noticed the link. He'd contacted the FBI to help the investigation into what was obviously a serial killer. The case had been handed over to the Special Crimes Unit, and Wren had chosen Adam to put together the Night Stalker's profile—white male working in a sales field, a loner in his mid to late twenties who lived somewhere in New England. Someone without connections who could come and go without suspicion.

The criminal profile had been circulated to every law enforcement agency in the northeast, but the Night Stalker remained at large. Bethany would have been his tenth victim. She fit the profile of his victims perfectly— emergency room nurse with dark hair and blue eyes, slight build, outgoing personality.

There was a difference, though.

Unlike the Night Stalker's other victims, Bethany worked at a small-town hospital. The other nurses had worked in city hospitals— Massachusetts General, Rhode Island Hospital, Brigham and Women's Hospital, Yale New Haven Hospital.

Whisper Lake Medical Center was a tiny hospital sitting on the outskirts of a tiny town. Its only claim to fame was the level-four trauma center that had been opened several years ago. Something about that bothered Adam, and he couldn't shake the feeling that they were missing something important.

"Even with the trauma center, it's still a small hospital in a small town," he murmured, reaching for a disposable cup and pouring coffee from the carafe a nurse had brought in hours ago. "I wonder why he changed his MO."

"You're not on the case," Wren reminded him.

"Just thinking out loud." He took a sip of the cold brew and grimaced.

"Why don't you go get us some hot coffee?" Wren suggested.

"I've already had too much of the stuff."

"You can't stay here forever, Adam."

"I can stay here until she wakes up."

"Then I hope River gets back from Boston soon. I hate cold coffee." She set her cup down.

"I thought River and Sam were on protection duty here at the hospital."

"They are. I sent River back to Boston this morning to double-check the ballistic results on the bullet they took from Charlotte."

"Why?"

"Because he's as much an expert as anyone working in the lab."

"That's not what I'm asking, and you know it. Why did you feel the need to have the ballistic results checked?"

"Because I'm wondering the same thing you are. Why the Night Stalker suddenly changed his MO. Why he chose a victim who worked in a small town at a small hospital. Before we pour more resources into this case, I want to make sure we're not dealing with a copycat—someone who had a bone to pick with Bethany and thought mimicking the Night Stalker would help him get away with murder."

"That's a stretch, Wren. Especially since the initial ballistics results are a match."

"River is going to give his own expert advice. And not just because I don't want to waste resources. Nine women are dead. When we catch their murderer, I want to make sure we have every *i* dotted and every *t* crossed. I don't want any doubts, any reason for a jury to hesitate."

Wren leaned forward, her suit jacket swinging open to reveal her holster. "It's not just about the case to me. I hope you know that, Adam. It's about seeing the victims get the justice they deserve. It's about seeing the survivors heal and move on."

Her phone buzzed and she pulled it from

her pocket, read a text message and then tucked it away again.

"River is back," she announced, standing and stretching her nearly six-foot frame. She was model-slender, her build belying the strength Adam had seen her use during self-defense training.

"And?"

"You're not on the case, so I shouldn't tell you."

"But you're going to," he guessed, and she nodded.

"The bullet taken from Charlotte matches the ones taken from the Night Stalker's victims. This is a go." She was suddenly all business, her dark eyes flashing with barely banked energy. "River is on the way up to the room. He'll be out in the hall. I have a meeting scheduled with Sam and some local and state law enforcement. Call me if she wakes up."

She was gone before he could respond.

He waited until she closed the door, then turned his attention back to Charlotte. She'd been his first love and his last. He'd walked away from her when she'd needed him most. He could do it again. It would be the easy choice: go back to Boston, pick up the case where he'd left off, let Wren, River and Sam handle things on this end.

That would require no emotional commitment, no trips down memory lane. No drives past the graveyard where Daniel's tombstone had been set. No visits to the cottage on the lake. It required him to do nothing but the job he'd been trained to do.

He couldn't do it, though.

He'd taken the easy path five and a half years ago. He'd failed Charlotte, and he'd failed himself. There was a big part of Adam that felt he'd also failed God. He hadn't been a Christian when he'd married Charlotte. They'd both been wild teens who'd lived by their own set of rules. Maybe if God had been part of what they'd been building together, the foundation would have been strong enough to withstand Daniel's death.

Still, Adam had taken vows.

He'd broken them.

In the years since, he'd learned what faith was. He'd learned what mercy and grace were. What he hadn't learned was how to forgive himself for what he'd done. He couldn't go back and change things, but he could do this.

He settled in the chair again.

"It's going to be okay, Charlotte," he said, patting her lax hand.

Her fingers moved—a tiny twitch that made his heart jump.

He waited, watching the rhythmic rise and fall of her chest beneath white hospital sheets, the flicker of her closed eyelids.

"Charlotte?" He touched her cheek, his palm resting against cool dry skin.

She opened her eyes.

He'd forgotten how beautiful her irises were—deep purple-blue rimmed with black. He'd forgotten how it felt to watch her wake, the haze of sleep slowly dissipating, the softness of her features sharpening.

"Why are you here?" she said, her voice raspy and raw, her eyes closing again.

"I thought it was time I was finally around when you needed me," he responded honestly, certain she'd already lost consciousness again.

"I don't need you," she whispered so quietly he almost didn't hear, and then she was unconscious again, the soft beep and hiss of machinery the only sounds in the quiet room.

He could have left then.

He'd done what he'd said he would. He'd stayed until she woke. She'd been lucid enough and aware enough to know who he was and to know she didn't want him around.

That shouldn't have hurt.

He told himself it didn't.

But there was a piece of his heart that still belonged to Charlotte. He might have failed her after Daniel died, but he wouldn't fail her now. Whether she needed him or not, he was there to stay until the Night Stalker was found and he knew for sure that she was safe.

TWO

Nine days.

That was how long Charlotte had been cooped up in the hospital. There'd been a steady stream of visitors during her stay. County police. Town sheriff. State police. FBI. All of them asking questions, most of which she couldn't answer.

She hadn't seen the face of the man who'd shot her.

She had seen his truck.

Just enough of it to know it was old. Big. A pickup with two doors.

She'd seen *him*, too. The man the FBI called the Night Stalker. She may not have seen his face, but she'd seen his height and breadth and the gleam of his eyes through the darkness.

She shuddered, pushing the image away.

She'd almost died.

Everyone who walked into the room reminded her of that.

Except for Adam. Her ex-husband. The one person she never would have expected to see sitting beside her hospital bed. In the earliest days of her recovery, she'd thought she was dreaming his presence, dreaming the shorter haircut, the fine lines near the corners of his eyes, the somberness in his gaze.

Only, Adam hadn't been a dream.

He'd been as real as the wound in her chest, the tube in her side, the surgical staples in her skin. The tube had come out. The wound was healing, the staples were gone, but Adam was still in Whisper Lake.

It still seemed impossible, but all she had to do was glance at the reclining chair he'd slept in the past few nights to know he'd really been there. He'd left his jacket lying across the arm, a duffel on the floor beside it. She wasn't sure where he'd gone, but she was certain he'd be back.

Charlotte's calm, predictable life had turned to chaos. She wasn't sure how it had happened or why. She only knew that she had to get things back on track. That meant going home to the cottage, sitting by herself, thinking through her options and making her own decision about where she wanted to go and what she wanted to do.

If law enforcement had its way, she'd be

taken to a safe house the minute she was discharged. Special Agent Wren Santino had outlined the plan for Charlotte earlier that day. They'd let her return home to collect a few personal items, and then they'd fly her out in a private jet, whisking her off to some destination only a few people were privy to.

And, of course, Clover would be with her.

That seemed to be the common theme. Everyone she spoke to about the FBI's plan had assured her that she could take her dog along. As if she were a child who would be persuaded by that. As if there'd ever been a doubt or question. *Of course* she'd bring Clover wherever she went.

If she went anywhere.

She had more than Clover to think about.

She had her teaching job at the community college, her dog-training class that met every Saturday morning. She had Bubbles to think about, too. Her neighbor wasn't getting any younger, and if Charlotte wasn't around, there'd be no one to keep an eye out for her.

The fact was, Charlotte had no reason to believe the Night Stalker knew who she was, where she lived or if she'd survived. Based on what she'd learned from Wren and Adam, she thought it was more likely that he'd gone on his merry way and was currently searching for a new victim somewhere far from Whisper Lake.

Of course, she wasn't law enforcement. She was just someone who'd been in the wrong place at the right time. Someone who'd gotten mixed up in something that had almost gotten her killed. She could be very wrong in her thinking. It was possible the serial killer did know who she was and where she lived. It was also possible that he planned to pay her back for ruining his plans to abduct his tenth victim.

She frowned. Maybe she did want to leave town for a while, go into hiding, let the FBI protect her.

Maybe.

But she needed to think about it, and the best place to do that was home.

She eased out of her hospital gown and into the loose-fitting jeans and sweater Bubbles had brought her. It took longer than it should have, and she was shaking when she finished, but she'd accomplished the task.

Now all she had to do was get home.

She thought about calling Bubbles and asking for a ride, but she didn't like the idea of her elderly neighbor driving out to the hospital at midnight. Besides, Bubbles had been spending her days at the cottage, taking care of Clover and sending away friends who'd been wondering why Charlotte hadn't shown up for meetings or training sessions. The FBI had coached her carefully, and Bubbles had told everyone who cared to know that Charlotte was on vacation. Unplanned. Spur of the moment. Just one of those things that young people did.

That was plenty for a woman in her eighties to deal with. She didn't need to be dragged out of bed at midnight to ride to Charlotte's rescue. Besides, if the Night Stalker was still out there, Charlotte didn't want Bubbles to be in his crosshairs.

She shivered, her thoughts going back to that moment on the road. The bright headlights. The dark form. The woman dropping to the ground.

The explosion of sound and of pain.

She'd been assured that she was safe. That the Whisper Lake Sheriff's Department was working with the state and federal police to keep her that way.

She believed she was safe.

But she was still afraid.

"That doesn't mean you're staying here," she muttered. "You're going home. You'll make decisions about whether to stick around once you're there."

"Are you okay, Charlotte?" someone called from the other side of the closed door.

Someone?

Adam. She knew his voice like she knew her own. Even after all these years.

"Charlotte?" he called again.

"I'm fine," she called back.

"Were you talking to someone?" The doorknob turned, the door opened and he was there. Standing in the threshold, his dark gray eyes a shade darker than she remembered, his hair just a little shorter. His shoulders were broader, too. The twenty-four-year-old kid he'd been had grown into his lanky frame.

"Just myself," she admitted, turning away so she wouldn't have to look into his eyes and see the concern and compassion there. Since they'd divorced, she hadn't spent much time thinking about how the years would change him. She'd been too busy trying to forget what they'd once had.

Now, though...

Now she could see what time had done. He was the same, but better. Calmer. Steadier. More patient. More willing to listen.

At night, when he thought she was sleeping, he'd sit in the recliner and read a leatherbound Bible, the thin pages rustling as he turned them. She'd wanted to ask him about that. She'd wanted to tell him about the church she'd joined and the comfort she'd found there. She'd kept silent, afraid to open doors that were better left shut. Her heart had been broken once. She wasn't sure she'd survive having it broken again.

"You still talk to yourself, huh?" She could hear his footsteps on the floor as he walked toward her, but she still wouldn't meet his eyes.

"Old habits are hard to break." She grabbed the bag of clothes and toiletries Bubbles had brought, wincing as the healing wound in her chest pulled tight.

"Let me." He took it from her hand, his fingers grazing her knuckles, his touch as familiar as sunrise. She could have leaned into it if she'd wanted to, leaned into him and let all the things that used to be wash over them. But they'd been divorced for longer than they'd been married. They were nothing more than strangers who had once known each other.

If she remembered that, she'd be just fine.

"Thanks."

"You look like you're planning to go somewhere," he commented as she grabbed her purse from the table beside the bed. Bubbles had brought that, too.

"I am."

"That's not a good idea, Charlotte."

"I don't see why not." She reached for a sheet of paper that lay on the table, the flowery stationery covered with a scrawled thank-you note from Bethany Andrews. Wren had delivered it in a plain white envelope. No hint of where it had come from or who had sent it. Charlotte had read the note several times already, the ER nurse's heartfelt thank-you reminding her that everything she'd been through had been worth it. Hopefully, they'd have a chance to meet face-to-face one day. She had a feeling she'd get along well with Bethany. She sounded like a sweet young woman.

Young? According to Wren, Bethany was twenty-five. Just three years younger than Charlotte. They'd attended Whisper Lake High School together for one year. Charlotte had ended her senior year six months pregnant, and she didn't remember much of her last year of high school except for the fact that she'd worn baggy shirts and oversize dresses, hoping to hide her growing belly.

Needless to say, she didn't remember Bethany.

She folded the note and slid it into her pocket, making the mistake of meeting Adam's eyes. He was watching, his shoulder against the wall, his expression neutral.

Whatever he was thinking, he hid it well.

"What?" she asked, breaking the silence because it felt too thick, too heavy and too filled with words that should have been said years ago.

"You're an intelligent woman, Charlotte. I'm sure you know exactly why leaving the hospital isn't a good idea."

"The Night Stalker doesn't know who I am. He doesn't know where I live, and as far as law enforcement can tell, he left town and hasn't returned."

"Law enforcement has no idea who he is or where he lives. For all anyone knows, he's your next-door neighbor."

"Bubbles is my only neighbor," she pointed out.

"I'm aware of that, Charlotte. We did live together for four and a half years."

She hadn't needed the reminder.

Sometimes when she couldn't sleep, she'd think about how it had felt to have someone lying in bed beside her. She'd remember what it was like to be wrapped in a solid embrace, or to reach out in the middle of the night, knowing that someone would reach back.

She missed that.

She was honest enough with herself to admit it.

"Wren said the Night Stalker probably hunted for his victims far away from home. If that's the case, he doesn't live anywhere near here," she commented.

"He changed his MO when he went after Bethany. He's always taken women from large hospitals. This time, it's different."

"That doesn't mean he lives close by."

"It doesn't mean that he doesn't," he pointed out.

She grabbed the Bible that Bubbles had brought to the hospital. The leather cover was cracked with age, the pages thin, wrinkled and highlighted with pink and yellow and lime green. Charlotte's grandmother had spent hours studying scripture. The Bible had been hers. In the years since Daniel's death, Charlotte had pored through it, seeking comfort in the words her grandmother had highlighted years ago.

She tucked it under her arm and reached for the slip-on shoes that Bubbles had set on a chair. "I don't know what you want me to say, Adam."

"I want you to say that you're going to follow the team's plan."

"What plan? The one where I get on a private jet and travel to an unknown destination?"

"Yes."

"Were you part of making it? Is that why you want me to agree to it?"

"You know I'm on leave," he said. "I have nothing to do with the plans that are made."

"I'm sure you'd like to be part of the decision-making process. You can go back to Boston and back to work," she replied and felt like an ogre for it. Adam had been nothing but kind, and she'd done nothing but try to push him away.

"No. I can't. Not until I know you're safe."

"I don't need you to keep me safe," she murmured, but her heart wasn't in the words. They sounded hollow and sad and a little lonely.

"I didn't say you did. I said I need to know you are. We might be divorced, but I still care about you, Charlotte. That has never changed."

She dropped one of the shoes. It bounced across the floor and slid under the bed.

"I'll get it," Adam said, grabbing her elbow when she bent to reach for it.

His fingers were warm, his skin calloused, and she could feel his touch long after he released his grip. She rubbed the spot, trying to wipe away the warmth and the memories that filled her head. Cold nights. Hot fires. Long conversations as they lay side by side.

He'd been her best friend.

He'd known everything there was to know about her.

And then he'd been gone.

She swallowed down grief that she shouldn't be feeling and whirled away, the quick movement making her light-headed.

She grabbed the doorjamb, her fingers curving around cool wood.

"You okay?" Adam asked, and she realized he had both of her shoes in his hand and was watching her.

"Fine. Just anxious to get out of here."

"For the record," he said, placing the shoes on the floor so she could slip into them, "I don't approve."

"Your disapproval is noted."

"But you're leaving anyway?"

"Yes."

"I'll get a wheelchair." He gave in with a lot less of a fight than she'd expected.

"I can walk."

"Suit yourself."

"I will." She stepped toward the door, and he touched her arm. Not stopping her. Just offering support. Her breath caught, her heart skipping a beat. His lashes were still long, thick and curly, his skin deeply tanned. He had a faint scar on his left jaw, and a solemnness to his demeanor that had been missing when he'd been a young deputy sheriff, fresh-faced and eager to prove himself. She felt dizzy with the memories, or maybe from moving too much and too quickly.

"On second thought," she murmured, "a wheelchair might be good."

He slipped his arm around her waist and led her to the recliner. She was sitting in it before she realized what was happening, his jacket settled around her, the scent of his cologne filling her nose.

"I'll be right back," he said, tucking a strand of hair behind her ear. He was looking into her eyes, and she was looking into his, and for a moment, there was nothing between them. No past. No pain. No heartache. They were simply two friends taking care of each other the same way they had since the first day they'd met.

He backed away, turning on his heels and striding from the room. Minutes later, he wheeled the chair in, helping her settle into it with the same quick efficient manner as any of the nurses or orderlies would have.

Whatever had been there was gone.

They were strangers again, and she told herself she was fine with it.

"Are you sure you want to do this?" he asked, and she nodded.

"Clover has been alone for eight nights. That's seven too many."

"He's a dog," he pointed out. "And Bubbles has been spending every day with him."

"He's family," she corrected.

He nodded, his dark eyes tracing the curve of her cheek and jaw. She could feel it like a physical touch.

Maybe they weren't so much like strangers, after all.

She frowned, relieved when he walked around to the back of the wheelchair and rolled her into the hall.

"One of my colleagues is waiting for us at the service entrance. We figured taking you out that way would attract a lot less attention than wheeling you through the lobby," he said. "You remember meeting Special Agent River Callahan?"

"Blond hair, blue eyes, nice smile?"

"I never paid much attention to the smile, but the other two are accurate. He and Wren are accompanying us to your place. They'll be staying there until you make a decision about protective custody."

"I don't remember agreeing to that."

"You didn't." His quick blunt response left no room for argument.

Not that she cared about that.

She could have argued.

She could have listed a dozen reasons why she didn't want or need federal officers in her house. Except that she wasn't a hundred percent sure she didn't need them.

She thought she didn't.

She hoped she didn't.

But if the Night Stalker really did live somewhere nearby, he might be someone she knew, someone who'd recognized her.

Someone who wanted to make sure that she didn't recognize him.

"Okay," she said.

"That was easy," he responded.

"You expected me to argue?"

"You're leaving the hospital against the advice of law enforcement," he pointed out, "so that seemed like a reasonable assumption."

"I'm tired of the hospital," she replied. "But I'm still really fond of being alive. If there's any chance the Night Stalker knows who I am—"

"We've been very careful about what information is released to the press."

"That doesn't mean much in a small town."

He didn't respond as he rolled her out into the hall.

She hadn't expected him to.

He might have moved to Boston, joined the

FBI, lived the high-stress busy life he'd always wanted, but he'd been born and raised in Whisper Lake. He knew how small towns worked, how information traveled over backyard fences and across church pews and made its way through the entire population so quickly it was nearly impossible to stop it. Regional papers had gotten wind of the Night Stalker's attempted kidnapping. They'd been fed information from anonymous sources who'd been happy to tell them that a woman had been shot saving a nurse from the serial killer. Charlotte had seen the story running on local and national television. It had been front-page news for a week, and there was no doubt that Whisper Lake was buzzing with it.

People who lived there knew the police had responded to a shooting near the lake. They knew there'd been two women at the scene. They knew everything except for the fact that Charlotte had been involved.

She wanted to keep it that way.

They reached the nurse's desk and the bank of elevators across from it. Adam passed both.

"Where are we going?" she asked, suddenly wondering if her escape from the hospital had seemed too easy because it was too easy.

Maybe Adam had his own plans.

Plans that didn't include letting her return to the cottage.

"To the freight elevator," he replied, turning down a quiet corridor that led deeper into the hospital.

"We are going home, right?" she asked as he stopped at the oversize elevator and tapped the call button.

"Yes."

"If you don't, I'll find a way to get there myself."

He leaned down, his lips so close to her ear, she thought she could feel their warmth. "I was a lot of things when we were married, Charlotte, but I was never a liar."

The doors slid open and he wheeled her into the cavernous space.

He didn't speak again, and she couldn't.

All the words were caught in her throat, a million memories of Adam and what he'd meant to her flitting through her brain and lodging in her heart.

When the doors slid open again, she inhaled deeply, the breath she hadn't realized she'd been holding puffing out into the chilly basement air. This part of the hospital wasn't one visitors normally saw. The cement floor was old and paint-spattered, track marks from thousands of carts being wheeled through etched into it. Up ahead, what looked like a wide garage door was illuminated by a few dim overhead lights.

A man waited there, his suit jacket crisp and neat, his expression grim. He had a holster beneath his sports coat. She'd seen it and him a lot during her hospital stay. He was a member of the FBI's Special Crimes Unit. He was also quiet, reserved and pointed in his questions. No matter how many times she answered, no matter what she said to him, she always had the idea that River Callahan didn't believe her.

He nodded as Adam wheeled her closer, pressing a button so the door rose. Beyond it, moonlight cast long shadows across a nearly empty lot. Like so many other places in Whisper Lake, the hospital was bordered by state land, the edge of a national forest just beyond the lot.

She couldn't take her eyes off the trees, off the circles of streetlights that illuminated the bare branches of old sycamores. Someone could be standing in the shadows, pointing a gun in her direction. She wouldn't know it until it was too late, until the bullet had already flown and she was lying on the ground, bleeding to death.

"It's okay," Adam said quietly as he pushed the wheelchair down a long ramp. "We've been keeping an eye on the area since you arrived. If anyone were out here, we'd know it."

"We?" River asked, his shoes tapping against the metal ramp.

"Figure of speech."

"Good. I was afraid you'd forgotten that you're currently on leave."

"That would be difficult to do, seeing as how you and Wren remind me several times a day," Adam replied. He sounded…older, more confident than he'd been five years ago.

And why wouldn't he?

Time had passed. Life had gone on. He'd created his new reality. She'd created hers. They hadn't spoken since the divorce papers were signed, their relationship cut off cold turkey as if they'd both understood that was how it had to be if they were going to move on without each other.

Cold air whipped across the parking lot, carrying a hint of wood-burning fires and pine needles. Winter would linger for another month or two. Then the world would blossom again. Charlotte planned to be around to see it. She planned to bring her dog-training group out on trails, to hike and fish and do all the things she did every spring and summer. She had to stay alive to do that. That was what she should be concentrating on. Not Adam and all the ways things were different. And the same.

She frowned, waiting impatiently as a black Cadillac drove around the corner of the building. It pulled up at the end of the ramp, and the next thing Charlotte knew, she was being bustled inside, nudged to the center of the back seat.

"When we reach your place, you'll have to walk. I don't want anyone seeing you in a wheelchair. We're sticking to the story about your vacation. People are going to want to hear all about it. We'll work on the details together. Okay?" Adam said as he slid in beside her.

She nodded.

The doors closed, and Adam grabbed her seat belt, pulling it across her lap and buckling it into place.

And then they were moving, the SUV pulling around the side of the building and out onto the highway, headlights gleaming on the paved road that led toward home.

He shouldn't have come.

That thought was crystal clear in Adam's mind, and he couldn't shake it. Not that coming hadn't been the right thing to do. It had been. The problem lay in the fact he couldn't make himself leave. Charlotte had turned the corner a week ago. She'd gone from critical to stable to ready for release. The hospital had held her an extra day at the FBI's request, and Adam had stayed by her side even then.

She was a habit he'd broken years ago.

Now he was forming it again.

That wasn't a good thing. It wasn't an acceptable one. He'd come to Whisper Lake because he'd needed to make amends for his failures. He hadn't come to reconnect with Charlotte or to fit himself back in her life.

They'd grown up and apart, and he'd been content with that.

He still was, but he couldn't help wondering if that would change. Enough time with Charlotte, enough quiet conversations in the middle of the nights, and maybe he'd begin to fall for her the way he had all those years ago.

Wren took the turn onto the country highway that led past the lake, and Charlotte slid toward Adam. His arm came up automatically, his fingers slipping around her shoulders, holding her steady.

"Careful," he cautioned. "You don't want to tear your wound open and end up back in the hospital."

"The wound is healing nicely. Tomorrow, I'll

see the surgeon, and he'll probably give me the go-ahead to get back to my regular activities."

"Tomorrow, huh?" he said, glancing at the rearview mirror. Wren met his eyes. Just like he knew she would.

"River, you want to contact headquarters and see if they can send someone out to check Charlotte's injury?" she asked.

"They don't need to send someone out," Charlotte argued. "As I said, I have an appointment with my surgeon. It's already been set up."

"You'll have to cancel," Wren said bluntly.

If the FBI had its way, Charlotte would be on a plane and out of the area before the scheduled appointment. Adam knew that. He wasn't sure Charlotte did.

"Look, I know you're doing your job and trying to protect me, but I really don't think I should stop living my life. If I do, people who know me will wonder why. They'll start asking questions. That will lead to speculation and gossip."

"Going to a surgeon who specializes in trauma is probably not the best way to keep your friends from asking questions," Adam cut in.

Charlotte frowned. "It's not like I'm going

to make an announcement about where I'm going. I have to go into work, and—"

"You're kidding, right?" he said, because there was no way she could really think that would be okay with anyone.

"I teach math at the community college, Adam."

"I'm aware of that." He wanted to add, "Congratulations," because she'd accomplished the goal she'd been shooting for since they were in middle school. He didn't, because she was angry. He could see it in the tightness of her jaw, feel it in the tension of her muscles.

"I can't just continue to not show up for work. My boss isn't going to be happy forever with the 'unexpected family emergency' excuse you guys provided," she continued.

"We spoke to your supervisor and the HR department," Wren said. "Your job is secure."

"I thought you didn't want anyone knowing what was going on?" Charlotte countered.

"We make exceptions when we have to. Your supervisor assured us that he'll keep the information private. He sent you his best."

"When did you contact Reggie?" Charlotte asked, her hands fisted so tight Adam was sure she was gouging her nails into her skin.

"A few hours ago," Wren answered, turning

onto another road, the beams of the car glancing across a raccoon that scurried out of sight.

"It would have been nice to be informed about it before now." Charlotte's voice was tight, her words clipped.

"My team has been busy making sure your property is secure. We've also been putting together a backup plan. In case this doesn't work."

"This?"

"You staying at home."

"I don't see why it wouldn't."

"Did you ever see yourself as the victim of a serial killer, Charlotte?" River finally cut into the conversation. As usual, when he spoke, what he had to say was right on point.

She shook her head, some of her tension easing, her hands relaxing. She understood what he was saying—that anything could happen in life, and that it was best to be prepared for it.

Adam could have explained that she already knew that.

Losing their son had taught them both the lesson.

The car fell silent as Wren navigated the deep curves. The darkness of the road made it difficult, and she drove slowly, easing around bends that Adam knew like the back of his hand. He knew the hilly areas, the blind entrances. He'd driven along this stretch of rural highway every day for nearly a decade. He hadn't forgotten it. Sure, the forest seemed lusher, the trees taller. Everything else was the same. The glint of lake in the distance. The pinpricks of house lights through dense foliage. Not many people lived out this far. Those who did liked their privacy.

Charlotte stared out the front window, her hands resting on her thighs, her gaze focused.

"What are you thinking?" he asked quietly.

She met his eyes, and he was caught in her gaze. Caught in that look of rebellion and pride that had drawn him to her when they were both outcast kids in a community that didn't quite understand them.

"That the road looks a lot darker than it ever has before," she responded.

They were nearing the crossroad that led to the cottage. She had to be remembering the way it had felt to see the truck, to hear Bethany scream.

He reached for her hand, the gesture more muscle-memory than planned. Her fingers curved through his, her palm as smooth and silky as he remembered.

He squeezed her hand gently, forced himself to release it.

"It's going to be okay," he said, and she nodded.

"That's the thing to say, right? When tragedy happens? How many times did we hear it after Daniel died?"

His entire body tensed, his blood seeming to freeze in his veins. He thought about Daniel plenty, but it had been years since he'd heard his name spoken aloud. Hearing it was like hearing the saddest melody ever written, reading the most heartbreaking ending of the most beautiful story ever penned.

"Too many," he managed to say.

The crossroad was just ahead, and he made himself focus on that—on the stop sign still strung with caution tape, the abandoned orange cones that had closed off the road after the shooting.

Something darted out from the trees, a blur of fur and legs, zipping toward the Cadillac with so much speed Adam was certain they'd hit it.

Wren slammed on the brakes, and he put his arm up to keep Charlotte from flying forward. As if the seat belt wouldn't hold her, as if it were somehow still his job to protect her.

The Cadillac skidded to the right, bumping a couple of sapling trees. Adam had his gun in hand before it stopped, his arm pressing Charlotte down and out of the line of fire.

He knew how quickly safety could turn to danger, and he knew how desperate the Night Stalker must be. The local papers had run the story. So had the *Boston Globe*, the *Providence Journal* and a half dozen other New England newspapers.

Guardian Angel Saves Tenth Victim of Notorious Night Stalker

Adam had seen that headline and a variation of it. The reporters might not have Charlotte's name, but they were speculating that she was someone local to Whisper Lake.

How long would it take the Night Stalker to figure out who she was and where she lived?

Would he try?

That was the question Adam had been asking himself. It was one he knew the team had been discussing.

"Holster your firearms," Wren said. "It was a dog."

"A dog?" Charlotte pushed his arm away and straightened, peering out the window. "What dog?"

"It ran off into the woods." Wren gestured

to the left. "Probably someone's pet got off the chain."

"We can't leave him. There are predators around here," Charlotte said.

"Yeah," River agreed. "And some of them are human and want you dead. How about we worry about that and let the owner find his own dog?"

"Or we could unroll the window and call to him," Charlotte argued. "It's not like we'd be out in the open. We'd just be sitting here exactly like we are. Only, we wouldn't be abandoning someone's pet to his fate."

"Fine. I'll give it two shouts. If he doesn't come, we're out of here." Wren unrolled her window. "Fido! Come!" she shouted.

Leaves rustled. A twig snapped.

A dog appeared.

At least, Adam thought it was a dog. It looked more like a giant ball of curly red fur. Floppy ears. Bearded snout. Dark eyes.

"Clover!" Charlotte shouted, and then she was scrambling over him, opening the door, tumbling out onto the road.

He grabbed the back of her soft pink sweater, hauling her up and into the SUV. Not caring about the injury or the incision. Not caring if they ended up back in the hospital getting her stapled up again.

All he cared about was keeping her alive.

If the dog loping toward them was hers, someone had let it out. Someone who might be waiting for her to return, waiting for her to go looking for the dog she obviously loved. Waiting on the road with a gun in hand, ready to finish what he'd begun.

Adam wanted to believe the Night Stalker didn't know Charlotte's identity, but he wasn't going to be foolish enough to ignore the possibility.

Wren obviously felt the same.

She shouted for River to jump out and get the dog, and then she was speeding toward the lake and the cottage and the memories Adam had tried so hard to forget.

THREE

The cottage door was open.

No lights on in the house.

No sign that anyone was there, but the door was wide-open and swaying slightly in the breeze. Charlotte had about two seconds to register that, and then Adam was moving, dragging her down onto the seat and covering her with his muscular body.

"What—" she began.

"Stay down," he commanded. "That door should not be open."

"You're right about that. We were here a couple of hours ago, and the place was clear and locked up tight," Wren said, her voice barely audible over the steady beat of Adam's heart. Charlotte could hear it thudding softly, feel the vibration through the soft fabric of his shirt.

She wanted to burrow in close, to take a little of the comfort she used to get from him.

But those years were over, and she tried to ease away, to put a little space between them.

"Stop," he said quietly, the words ruffling the hair near her temple. "Just wait until we're sure there's no one inside. Where's Sam, Wren? Wasn't he supposed to be here?"

"At the airport picking up Honor. She brought the security equipment I wanted. I figured between you, me and River, we'd be fine until they arrived."

"I shouldn't be included in that. I'm on leave," Adam said, and Wren snorted.

"Now you realize it? Stay here. I'm going to check out the interior of the house."

She didn't sound very concerned.

Maybe Charlotte shouldn't be, either, but her pulse was racing, her heart hammering against her ribs.

"That's not policy," Adam responded, his voice vibrating through his chest and straight into Charlotte's ear.

"And?" Wren said, opening her door.

Cold air swept into the vehicle, carrying the sound of leaves whispering and water lapping against the shore. *Home*, they seemed to say.

"If you break policy, I'll have to write you up. That's one of your rules, remember? We all follow protocol. It's the only way to assure the safety of the team," Adam said.

"Since when do you quote my rules?" Wren muttered.

"Since you spent nine days reminding me that I was on leave and not a working member of the team," he responded.

"Here are the facts. I'm here. You're here. That door is open. One of us needs to check the house. Since you're currently in the back seat protecting our witness, that will have to be me. My guess is Bubbles was here after we left. She probably fed the dog and accidently left the door open."

"Bubbles would never leave a door open," Charlotte offered. "She's paranoid."

That was a slight exaggeration, but Bubbles really did worry about someone breaking into her house. She locked her doors and windows and checked them five times before she went to bed at night. She'd told Charlotte to do the same.

You can't be too careful was one of her favorite sayings.

Careful didn't mean leaving a door open.

"She's also elderly," Wren said. "Sometimes that brings a little bit of forgetfulness. Even to the sharpest mind. You two stay here. I'll check out the house."

She probably would have closed the door

and walked away, but a dog barked, the sound mixing with twigs snapping, paws scrabbling, feet pounding on packed earth.

There was a flurry of movement, a half second when Charlotte wondered if they were under attack, and then Clover was springing over the front seat, his furry face pressed close to hers, his tongue lolling out.

"How did you get here?" she asked, and he smiled in the way only a dog could.

"He must have known you were in the car. He took off through the trees and headed this way. Never veered from his course," River said, opening up the passenger door and peering in.

"Since you're here, I'll go inside with Wren." Adam moved away, taking all his warmth with him.

"Good idea. You've lived here. You know the house. I'd like to see it through your eyes and get an idea of where the most likely security breaches will be," Wren said. She was moving away from the vehicle, heading for the front porch of the cottage with a confident stride that seemed to say she really did think the house was empty.

Charlotte hoped she was right.

She wasn't as convinced.

She knew Bubbles. Age hadn't made her more forgetful. It had made her more obsessive.

"I'll be back soon," Adam said quietly as he climbed out of the car. "Stay here and do exactly what River says."

He walked away quickly, his long legs eating up the ground way faster than hers ever could. He'd been six inches shorter when they'd met, but still taller than every kid in seventh grade. She'd noticed him because of his height and because he was the only biracial kid in school. Whisper Lake wasn't known for its diverse population. Nor was it known to be tolerant of people like Adam's mother. Darla Whitfield had ended up in Whisper Lake by default. Her then-boyfriend had moved there when he'd taken a job for the United States Forest Service. When he'd left for another job, she and Adam had stayed in the single-wide trailer they'd been renting. Darla had worked as a waitress and changed boyfriends faster than she'd changed hair color. Which, according to people who'd known her back then, had been a lot.

That had been years before Charlotte had met Adam, but she'd always imagined him as a scrawny five-year-old, running wild on the ten-acre property that the trailer sat on. By the time she'd moved to town, he'd gotten a part-time job to help pay the bills and was working almost as much as his mother.

He'd wanted better for his kids. He'd wanted them to have happy childhoods, to grow up feeling secure and safe and valued. He'd told Charlotte that long before she'd found out she was pregnant. After, he'd been even more determined. He'd applied for and gotten a job with the Whisper Lake Sheriff's Department; he'd attended college. When he hadn't been doing either of those things, he'd been home being the best father anyone could be.

And then Daniel was gone, and all the dreams and hopes seemed to be gone with him. Adam had changed after that. In the six months that preceded him leaving, he'd spent more time away from Charlotte than with her. When he'd been home, they'd tiptoed around each other, afraid to break the silence that had filled the cottage since Daniel's death.

She shivered, pulling her thoughts back to the present.

River had taken a position outside the car, his back to Charlotte. She looked past him, watching as the windows in the cottage lit up. There were no gunshots, no loud warnings. Just the silence of the lake at night, the soft sheen of moonlight reflected on the water, the swish of the breeze through the trees.

Beside her, Clover panted quietly, his head resting on her thigh, his body relaxed. If someone were lurking outside the car, he'd know it. She wanted to relax, too, but the night seemed as still and silent as it had been the night she'd heard Bethany scream.

That scared her.

She got out of the car, restless and worried and not sure why.

"You should probably get back in the vehicle," River said without glancing her way.

"There's no one out here but us," she countered. "If there was, Clover would let me know."

As if on cue, Clover jumped out of the car, his head bumping her hand as he moved in close. His attention was on the lake, his nose pointed to the air as he sniffed several times.

He whined and would have darted away, but she caught his collar and pulled him back.

"Down!" she commanded, and he dropped onto his stomach, his nose still in the air.

He'd caught the scent of something or someone, and that was enough to make Charlotte back up. She hadn't survived a gunshot wound to the chest to die in her front yard because she hadn't heeded her dog's warning. She planned to get in the car, pull the door closed and wait for Adam and his associates to deal with whoever might be out there, but Clover barked, the sound the same high-pitched greeting he offered when friends came to visit.

If someone was out there, it was someone he knew.

"Who is it, Clover?" she asked as if the dog could answer.

He barked again, his tail swiping back and forth across the pavement. His scruff wasn't raised. He wasn't growling. He sensed a friend, and the only one who lived anywhere nearby, the only person who would possibly be out at this time of night, was Bubbles.

"Bubbles!" she called, her voice echoing loudly in her ears.

"Get back in the car," River said, taking her arm and trying to urge her into the vehicle.

"I think Bubbles is out there," she responded, shrugging away. Clover was still staring at the lake, his tail wagging, his tongue out.

"Maybe it's Bubbles. Maybe it's not. How about you let us figure it out?" River edged into her space, and she found herself stepping backward, her calves knocking against the door frame.

She would have gotten in and let him close the door, but Clover jumped up and sprinted away.

"Clover!" she shouted, brushing past River as she ran after the dog.

She could see him racing toward the lake, his red coat black in the moonlight, his tail high.

She sprinted after him, her legs weak from too many days in a hospital bed, her body aching from trauma, surgery and over a week of being sedentary. She was used to moving. She ran, hiked, biked and camped. She'd always been fast, but after Daniel's death she'd become faster. Running had been her escape. Now she had other things. Clover and dog training and her visits to the hospitals and Alzheimer's facilities. She still ran, though, because expending herself physically was sometimes the only way to quiet her thoughts.

Despite the training, despite the hours that she'd spent running, she felt like she was moving through mud, her pace slow and uneven, her breath shallow and labored.

"Clover!" she called again as the dog splashed into the winter-cold lake water.

"Come!" she commanded, but he was on a scent, and he didn't stop.

She had no idea what he'd seen, smelled or

heard. All she could see was his dark head bobbing as he swam. The inky water stretched out in every direction, Bubbles's ancient dock jutting out toward the center of it. If someone was there, they were well hidden.

Or they were in the water on the other side of the dock.

The thought filled her head and wouldn't leave it.

Before Daniel drowned, she'd spent hours every summer swimming in the lake. She'd gone canoeing and fishing there. Since his death, she'd avoided it. She didn't swim, and when she wanted to canoe, she drove to another section of the lake. She knew she was being irrational, the lake and the water were no different than they'd ever been, but she still hated the undulating waves, the dark surface, the sooty root-filled bottom. The thought of even sticking her toe in it filled her with dread. She couldn't imagine jumping in, allowing her head to go under and water to surround her.

She ran toward the dock, hoping to cajole Clover out of the water. Her foot hit an old tree stump, and she tripped, flying forward so quickly she'd have landed on her face if River hadn't grabbed the back of her sweater.

"Thanks," she panted, catching her balance, her focus still on Clover.

"Anytime," Adam replied.

Surprised, she stumbled again, and he hooked an arm around her waist, pulling her into his side.

"How about you don't fall and break something while we're out here?" he muttered as he helped her onto the dock. "I don't think either of us wants to spend any more time in the hospital."

"I don't intend to break anything. I intend to get my dog out of the lake before he drowns."

"Isn't he some sort of poodle mix?" he asked, moving cautiously out onto the rickety dock.

"Yes."

"Then I'm sure he can get himself out."

"The water is freezing, and—"

"He's a dog," he said calmly, "and you'd have been wiser to get back in the car when River told you to."

"He's more than a dog. He brought me out of the depression I was in after Daniel died. He filled up some of the empty space that was left after—" *You walked out.*

She didn't finish.

"What I meant is that most dogs can swim

and most won't stay in freezing water for very long. Once he gets cold, he'll head back."

"I hope you're right," she said, turning her attention back to Clover. He was still swimming, his head bobbing above the water a dozen yards away. She tracked his trajectory, trying to figure out where he was heading and why he'd be going there. He did love water, but it wasn't like him to refuse a direct command.

"Clover, co—"

The words choked off as she spotted something a few feet in front of Clover. White fabric floating languidly. White hair drifting on the black water. A white hand beneath the surface.

Her brain wouldn't put words to what she was seeing, but her body knew. Someone was in the water. Facedown. Lifeless.

She was in the lake before she realized what she was doing, swimming toward the prone figure. By the time she reached it, Clover was there, his mouth filled with the gauzy fabric as he tried to tug the person through the water.

"Good boy," Charlotte said, her teeth chattering, her fingers nearly numb as she wrapped her arm around a scrawny chest and tugged the person's head out of the water.

She saw the face, the hair, the bright red lipstick smeared across the wrinkled lips.

"Bubbles," she murmured, sliding her nearly frozen fingers to her friend's jugular and praying she'd find a pulse. Her fingertips seemed frozen, but she was sure she felt Bubbles's heart beating.

"Pulse?" Adam asked, and she realized he was right beside her, standing shoulder-deep in water.

"Yes. Faint, but there."

"Is she breathing?" He slid an arm under Bubbles, taking her weight from Charlotte.

"I don't know."

Or maybe she just didn't want to know.

She'd been watching Bubbles's chest, waiting to see it rise and fall. She'd seen nothing but soaked cotton fabric lying still against her friend's narrow sternum.

"We need to get her back to shore," he said, supporting Bubbles's neck as he maneuvered through the water.

Charlotte glided through his icy wake, her muscles cramping from cold. She tried not to think about what she was doing, tried not to focus on the water or the way it lapped against her arms and legs as she moved. Since Daniel's death, the lake had become almost a living thing to her, its attributes evil and ugly.

Her feet touched the bottom and she waded toward shore, Clover paddling beside her. He seemed content to stay there now that he'd found what he'd been looking for.

By the time they reached the pebbly beach, Adam was performing CPR, Wren beside him, her fingers curved around the delicate bones of Bubbles's wrist.

Charlotte dropped down near Bubbles's head, brushing wet hair from her cheek.

"You're going to be okay," she said, as if her words could make it true. "Is she breathing?"

"Not yet," Wren responded, shrugging out of her coat and laying it over Bubbles. "River called for an ambulance. He's gone back to the road to flag them in."

"I don't understand how this could have happened. She swims three seasons out of the year. Almost every day."

"She's in her eighties. No matter how good of shape she's in, her reflexes aren't what they used to be. She was probably on the dock, tripped and fell in. The water is cold. It wouldn't have taken long for her to lose some muscle function," Wren replied, nudging Adam to the side. "I'll take over rescue breathing. You take Charlotte back to the house and get her warm."

"I'd rather stay here." She could hear sirens. She knew the ambulance was on the way.

He didn't argue, just dropped his arm around her shoulders and pulled her into his side. If he'd been a stranger, it would have been a totally inappropriate thing to do. She was aware of that. Just like she was aware of the warmth that seeped through her soaked sweater, of the way her pulse leaped at his touch.

He was her ex-husband, but he'd once been her best friend.

When he was this close, when his warmth was seeping into her, chasing away the chill, she could almost forget that he wasn't anymore.

She eased away, touching Bubbles's hair again.

Clover barked, the sharp quick warning making her jump. She swung toward him, saw that he was staring toward Bubbles's house, his nose in the air, his hackles up.

"What—"

She didn't get a chance to finish.

Something flashed in the darkness, and Adam tackled her to the ground with so much force the air left her lungs. She was flat on her back, Adam pressing her into the rocky ground as the earth exploded, bits of sand and rock raining down on her face.

They should have expected this.

Adam should have expected it.

He hadn't, and it had almost cost Charlotte her life.

He raced up the beach and sprinted into Bubbles's yard, staying in the shadows of the overgrown bushes that lined her property. He knew the yard well. Years ago, he'd been the one to mow it. She'd offered him the job when he was twelve, and he'd taken it because he'd seen his mother's electric bill and knew their power was about to be shut off. Again.

Once a week, all summer long, he'd walk to Bubbles's house, take out her old lawn mower and cut the grass. She'd hand him icy glasses of lemonade and crisp ten-dollar bills and tell him that he was going somewhere in his life.

She'd been the closest thing to a grandmother he'd ever had. She'd taught him to value himself and other people. Because of her encouragement, he'd finished high school and he'd attended college. When he was around her, she forced him to be his better self.

When he'd left Whisper Lake and Charlotte, he'd left Bubbles, too. He hadn't realized how much he'd missed her until he'd seen her in Charlotte's hospital room. He hadn't realized how much he regretted not keeping in touch until he'd pulled her body from the lake.

If she died before he had a chance to thank her for all she'd done...

He winced away from the thought, his focus on the gravel driveway that emptied out onto the country road. Sirens were screaming, masking other sounds. The perp could have been crashing through the bushes that edged the property, and Adam wouldn't have been able to hear it.

He didn't think that was the case, though.

He thought the shooter was gone, slipping away the same way he'd come—silently.

The Night Stalker was notorious for staying out of sight. The Special Crimes Unit had obtained security footage from several of the hospitals where victims had been abducted. The unit's tech expert, Honor Remington, had spent weeks poring over images of a hooded man who'd been seen on several of the videos. Despite her best efforts, his face remained hidden, always turned just slightly away from the cameras, his hood shadowing his features.

If the Night Stalker had just fired a shot at Charlotte, he wouldn't be standing out in the open waiting to be discovered. He'd be running for his lair, going back to the place where he hid with his victims.

Still, Adam moved cautiously, walking along the edge of the driveway, searching for signs that a vehicle had been there. He hit pay dirt, his attention caught by deep gouges in the gravel. Tire tracks. They'd been made by a vehicle that was moving quickly, the tires spinning and spitting chunks of gravel in every direction.

He pulled his phone out of his pocket. It was wet but functional, and he sent a text to River, filling him in and asking him to keep the ambulance and its crew away from Bubbles's property.

They'd need to get an evidence team out here. One a little better prepared than the local police department.

He doubted there'd be tread marks in the gravel, but the width and depth of the tracks could be measured and inputted into a data bank that would compare them to track marks left by other vehicles. If they were fortunate, they'd get a match that would give them some idea of the kind of vehicle that had been used.

He moved back toward the house, staying parallel to the lake shore. He was certain he knew where the shooter had been standing when he'd fired the shot—the cleared area just beyond Bubbles's back deck. There were no bushes or trees there, nothing to block her view of the lake. It was the perfect spot to sit and watch the sun set. It was also the perfect vantage point for a sniper.

It seemed odd that the Night Stalker would go to this kind of effort to silence Charlotte. Up until now, he'd stayed a step ahead of law enforcement by kidnapping his victims and holding them prisoner for weeks or months before he killed them. After they were dead, he transported them back to the area he'd taken them from. The victims had all been found beside roads that were close to the hospitals they'd been taken from. Aside from a few synthetic fibers found on three of the victims, there was no evidence leading in any direction, no way of knowing where the victims had been or where they had been murdered. Everything Adam knew about the Night Stalker made him believe that the serial killer would go deep into hiding at the first sign of trouble. Based on that, Adam had assumed that he was nowhere near Whisper Lake. He'd obviously assumed wrong.

But then, the Night Stalker had acted out of character from the very beginning of this case. He'd kidnapped a woman from a small regional hospital. He'd used a chloroformed rag to knock Bethany out, but he hadn't taken the time to make sure she'd stay out. The rag had been found in the parking garage, dropped and forgotten by someone who'd obviously been rushing. Finally, after years of stalking and preying on women, the killer had made mistakes. Those mistakes had been the reason Bethany had escaped.

What Adam hadn't been able to figure out was why the Night Stalker had been in a hurry. Adam had spent a lot of time studying the previous cases. He'd put together a criminal profile that he believed was as close to an accurate picture of the man as they could get without meeting him. The Night Stalker was a confident criminal who believed he was too smart to make mistakes, too intelligent to ever be found out. He planned abductions carefully, stalking his victims until he knew their routines, their vehicles, their schedules.

He'd managed to kidnap nine women from hospital parking garages without anyone seeing or hearing anything. He had his methods down cold. Somehow, though, he'd failed with Bethany. He'd managed to get her into her car and drive her out of the parking garage. He'd transferred her to his truck while she was still unconscious. If he'd followed his normal pattern, he'd have transported her somewhere, raped her, tortured her, kept her until he tired of her and then killed her.

Instead, she'd come out of her chloroform-induced stupor and jumped out of the vehicle when her abductor slowed at a stop sign. It was a huge mistake. One that would, hopefully, lead to his capture.

But why had he made it?

That was the question Adam couldn't stop asking himself, the one that kept him up at night, that made him pace the hospital room while Charlotte had slept. Something had thrown the Night Stalker off his stride.

If they could figure out what, they might be able to find him.

Adam stepped into the clearing, probing the deep shadows near the corners of the house. He wasn't expecting to see anyone, but he hadn't expected someone to take a potshot at Charlotte, either.

If the dog hadn't barked, if Adam hadn't glanced toward Bubbles's house, if he hadn't seen a shadow moving across the landscape, Charlotte would be dead, and he'd be living with the guilt of knowing that his mistake had allowed it to happen.

He already knew how that felt—grief compounded a hundredfold by the knowledge that different choices might have changed the tragedy. He'd been the one to suggest he and Charlotte go out to dinner and leave Daniel with a sitter. He'd been the one who'd insisted that everything would be just fine. He'd been wrong. Daniel had died because of it.

He moved across the yard, his gaze shifting to the lake. The vista was as beautiful as he remembered—clear starry night, inky water sprinkled with moonlight, the lights of the town twinkling through the trees on the far shore. It was the people on the beach below that he was interested in, though. He could see them clearly—Wren leaning over Bubbles, Charlotte lying prone beside her. Clover sitting with his face turned to Bubbles's house. The gunman had had a great view and an easy shot.

Had he known that before he arrived?

Was he familiar with this property, this view?

Adam had been on the Night Stalker's trail for three years. He knew everything there was to know about the killer's MO. The Night Stalker was intelligent. He was patient. He was meticulous. In his day-to-day life, he was probably a law-abiding, hardworking citizen. A bit of a loner, but not someone neighbors would worry about. He was the kind of guy who'd wave from across the street, smile and have pleasant conversations when he ran into people he knew.

He had a veneer of respectability that kept him safe.

He knew it, so why take risks by hanging around in a town as small as Whisper Lake? A town where everyone knew everyone and strangers were always noticed?

Unless he belonged there.

Unless he was as much a part of Whisper Lake as Charlotte and Bubbles.

The thought shivered through Adam, and he couldn't shake it. If it were true, everything changed. There would be no more speculating about what the Night Stalker would do, whether he would go after Charlotte or go into hiding. If he lived in town, the likelihood that he knew Charlotte was high. Even if he didn't know her, he could easily find out who she was. A drive down the road where he'd shot her, a look at the mailboxes. A question asked here or there, and he'd have her identity as well as the fact that she was divorced, living alone, her only neighbor an elderly widow.

An ambulance crew had arrived. He could see them making their way toward the beach, jogging across grass and sand, equipment bouncing in their hands.

To his left, branches broke as someone

stepped through the thick line of bushes that edged Bubbles's property. He didn't pull his firearm. There was no way the Night Stalker would be bold enough to step out into the moonlight.

As he watched, River stepped into view, his coat opened to reveal his holster and firearm. Unlike most of the members of the Special Crimes Unit, River hadn't been recruited from within the ranks of the FBI. He'd been a detective with the LAPD, a decorated war veteran and a well-known ballistics and blood-splatter expert. He'd been used as an expert witness in dozens of trials, and he was as good on the stand as he was in the field.

From what Adam had heard, River had been Wren's top pick when she'd begun assembling her team. They had a history together—military careers that had crossed a few years before they'd retired.

Adam didn't know the story. He hadn't asked. Most members of the team were younger and less experienced. Gung ho and capable, but still earning their stripes. River and Wren were the exception. They'd made names for themselves long before they'd entered the FBI.

"Find anything interesting?" River asked,

his gaze shifting from Adam to the beach and back again.

"Aside from tracks in the gravel? Not yet," Adam replied.

"I took a look at them and snapped a few pictures. Just in case."

"In case what?"

"The clouds roll in and a storm blows through and the evidence disappears."

"Do you have an ETA for the evidence team?"

"The state wants to send their team in. Wren wants ours. Not sure if they plan to flip a coin or duke it out. One way or another, I hope they come to an agreement quickly. I'm anxious to input any information they collect into our data banks. The tracks are deep. I'm thinking they were made by a truck."

"Late-model and two-door?" Adam said, and River smiled grimly.

"That would be my guess. We'll see what the team turns up. How's the old lady?"

"Hopefully healthy enough to resent being called that."

"She didn't look good when she was in the lake. Wren said she had a pulse?"

"She did."

"Did you see any visible signs of trauma?"

FOUR

The ambulance had parked at the end of Charlotte's driveway, its flashing lights splashing across gravel and grass as two EMTs lifted Bubbles into the vehicle. She didn't move, didn't open her eyes, didn't seem to be at all aware that she was being taken to the hospital.

She was breathing on her own, though.

That was good news.

Please, God, let her be okay.

The prayer whispered through Charlotte's mind, and she wanted to believe that God would hear and that He'd answer by allowing Bubbles to fully recover.

That was what Charlotte *wanted* to believe, but she'd learned the hard way that God didn't always answer the way she wanted or expected.

She'd prayed desperately in the hours after Daniel had wandered away from his babysit- She'd bargained with God, offering her

River asked, his attention shifting to the beach again.

"No, but I didn't have time to look very closely."

"We'll have to make sure the medical team does due diligence. If they find bruises or defensive wounds, we'll need to know about it."

"You think she was attacked?"

"I think it's odd that she ended up in the lake the night Charlotte was returning home," River responded. "The fact that someone was up here playing sniper while you were down on the beach trying to save Bubbles is even more suspicious. I've never believed in coincidence. Even if I did, I wouldn't believe this was one."

He was right, and if Adam hadn't been busy reacting to crises, he'd have already been thinking in that direction.

"Did you call the local police department? We need to have someone at the hospital when Bubbles arrives."

"I did one better. I called Sam. He and Honor are heading to the hospital. He'll stay there. She'll drive here with the security equipment."

"We may not need it. If the Night Stalker is sticking around, Charlotte is going to have to leave. Wren should be able to have a safe location ready within a few hours."

River snorted. "Do you think you can convince Charlotte to go?"

"The bullet came within a couple inches of her."

"And?" River walked to the driveway, and Adam followed.

"Charlotte isn't a risk taker." At least, she hadn't been. A lot of years had passed since they'd been married. They'd both changed. Maybe she'd become more willing to take chances. Maybe she was no longer afraid of spiders or disgusted by the thought of eating hard-boiled eggs. Maybe she'd learned to rub her stomach and pat her head at the same time, or discovered the perfect recipe for fudge.

There were dozens of things he had once known about her that might no longer be true.

He'd spent nine days by her side. He'd noticed all the little ways she'd physically changed, but there were other subtler changes, too. Her smile wasn't as open. Her gaze wasn't as direct. She was less likely to speak and more likely to listen.

"She might not be a risk taker, but she's a homebody and a fighter. She'll want to stick close to the cottage and the lake, and I think she'd rather face this guy head-on than hide from him."

"You might be right," Adam conceded. "But

what she wants isn't as important as [...] her alive. We know what the Night S[...] capable of. He's already made two [...] on her life. He's not going to stop [...] succeeds."

"Or until he's caught."

They'd reached the end of the drivew[...] River gestured toward the road. "Wher[...] this go?"

"It's a ten-mile track from the crossr[...] an old logging camp that shut down in th[...] ties." He'd explored the area when he w[...] kid, ducking into old shanties that still s[...] against the backdrop of the encroaching forest.

"Are there any side roads between here and there?"

"None," Adam answered, suddenly u[...] standing exactly what River was gettir[...] The shooter had driven in. He had to[...] driven out. "Did a vehicle pass you wh[...] were waiting for the ambulance?"

"No, and I would have noticed if o[...] was standing in the middle of the ro[...]

"So, he drove toward the loggin[...] Adam said more to himself than to[...]

"Let's see if we can find him." [...] off, and Adam followed, sprinting [...] cottage and the Cadillac.

time, her money and her resources in exchange for her son's life.

In the end, she'd been left heartbroken.

She was older now, more mature. She understood what she hadn't then—God's plan didn't always mean easy paths. A year after Daniel's death, she'd attended church. Not for Christmas or Easter. Not because someone had asked her to go. She'd attended because she'd wanted answers. She'd needed to know if God was really there, if He existed. If He cared.

She'd found Him.

She'd found pieces of herself.

But she'd never forgotten that God didn't bargain. Not even with desperate mothers who promised Him everything.

"Please, not this time," she whispered as she jogged to the ambulance, Clover prancing beside her.

"Can I ride along?" she asked the EMT.

"Are you family?"

"I'm the closest thing she has to one."

"All right, but your dog has to stay here."

"Can you bring him into the cottage?" She tossed the question over her shoulder, knowing that Wren was right behind her.

"You can do it just as easily, because there is no way you're going to the hospital."

She turned, surprised and a little disoriented. She'd spent five and a half years on her own. She made decisions, did her own thing and didn't rely on anyone for help. "What's that supposed to mean?"

"Exactly what it sounds like. You're not going," Wren said. No heat in her voice. No emotion. Just a statement of fact.

"You're kidding, right?"

"Why would I be?"

"I don't need your permission to go to the hospital." She stepped away from the ambulance, though. She didn't want to do anything that would postpone Bubbles getting the care she needed. Arguing with Wren while the ambulance crew waited would do that.

"We're ready to roll. Are you coming?" the EMT asked, and she shook her head.

"Good choice," Wren said as the ambulance doors shut and it sped away.

"Just because I didn't ride in the ambulance doesn't mean I'm not going to the hospital." She headed toward the house, determined to put Clover inside, get in her Jeep and go.

She reached the Cadillac, its passenger doors still open, and grabbed her bag and purse from the back seat. She'd need her ID, her keys and her cell phone. She was still soaked, her skin so cold she couldn't feel the chill anymore. Smart would be getting changed before she left, grabbing a coat and gloves and maybe even a hat.

Instead, she opened the front door, let Clover into the entry and closed it again.

"Going somewhere?" Adam asked.

She jumped, swinging around so quickly she felt dizzy.

"You just scared ten years off my life," she breathed, her hand pressed to her chest, the skin aching.

"Sorry about that," he responded, his gaze cold and a little hard. "Wren said you want to go to the hospital."

"Wren is correct."

"You know that's not a good idea, Charlotte."

"No, I actually don't know that."

"Someone just tried to kill you," he responded. "Isn't that proof enough that you shouldn't be out in public places?"

"It's proof, but it doesn't change anything. Bubbles is one of my closest friends. She's been here for me when no one else was."

Something shifted in his eyes, the coldness replaced by what looked like sorrow. "Charlotte—"

"I didn't mean you," she cut in. She didn't want to hear whatever he planned to say. She didn't want to know if he had regrets, if he wished he could go back and change things.

She'd loved Adam for so many years it had been difficult to learn how to not love him. She'd done that, though. Done it and tried to forget what it was like to have someone care like Adam had. Now he was back, fitting into her life as perfectly as he always had, and all the memories of what they'd been were still there.

"Who else would you mean?" he asked, touching her cheek the way he used to every morning before he left for work, fingers drifting to her nape and kneading the tense muscles there. "We were everything to each other. I haven't forgotten that."

"Adam—"

"I need to go, but I want you to promise me you won't leave the cottage while I'm gone." He traced a line from her nape to the hollow in her throat, his finger resting there for a moment. Her pulse beat wildly, and it wasn't because of fear or anger or any of the other emotions she could and should be feeling.

It was because he was an arm's length away, and if she'd wanted to, she could have taken a step closer, let her hands settle on his waist, fit herself to him the way she used to.

"Promise me, Charlotte," he murmured,

leaning down and kissing her forehead, his lips warm, the contact light and undemanding.

And she could feel herself melting, sinking into him the way she always had.

"Okay," she responded, and he nodded, his hand dropping away as he stepped back.

"Wren will stay here with you. Another member of our team will arrive shortly. I'll be back as soon as I can."

"Where are you going?" she finally thought to ask, her brain starting to function again, her heartbeat slowing as he moved away.

He didn't answer, and she would have followed him down the porch stairs and into the driveway, but Wren stepped between them, taking her arm and pulling her toward the door.

"Inside," she said grimly, opening the door and nudging Charlotte into the entryway.

"What's going on?"

"Nothing you need to worry about."

"Saying that is only making me worry more."

"We have a handle on things. All you need to do is stick with the plan."

"I didn't know there was one."

"You just agreed to it. You stay inside. We find the guy who wants to kill you."

"I didn't agree…" But, of course, she had.

She'd looked into Adam's eyes, felt the warmth of his hand against her skin, and she'd promised that she'd stay in the house while he was gone.

"That was sneaky," she muttered.

"What?" Wren asked, walking into the kitchen and checking the lock on the window before she closed the shades.

"Adam…" She shook her head. She wasn't going to go into all the details of what he'd done. She was sure Wren had seen and heard it all. She'd probably put him up to it.

"You think he manipulated you?" Wren asked, turning to face her. She didn't look annoyed. She didn't look amused. She looked curious.

"He did."

"He didn't," Wren corrected, her dark eyes filled with sympathy and understanding. "He cares about you. The way he acted was a result of that, so if you think that he used your relationship to get you to cooperate, you're thinking wrong."

"Relationship? He's my ex-husband."

"And?" Wren walked into the living room, checked the windows there and pulled the curtains closed.

"We don't have a relationship."

"Can I ask you a question and get an honest answer?" Wren said, dropping into the recliner, her long legs stretching out in front of her. She had the tall lean look of a runway model, her hair always perfectly styled, her makeup understated and impeccable, but there was something comforting about her, too—a nurturing vibe that probably put most people at ease.

Charlotte hadn't been nurtured as a kid, though. Her mother had been more interested in partying than parenting. Even before she'd divorced Charlotte's father, she'd been on a mission to find herself and whatever faux joy that brought her. Charlotte's father had been just as focused on himself, pursuing his real estate career with more passion than he'd ever pursued parenting. When they'd split, she'd landed on her grandparents' doorstep, because neither parent wanted the responsibility of raising a teenager.

So yeah, being nurtured wasn't something Charlotte had ever looked for or needed, and she couldn't help wondering what Wren's game was, what she hoped to accomplish by acting sympathetic and caring.

"That depends on the question," she finally responded, grabbing a towel from the linen closet in the hall and wrapping herself in it.

She was colder now than she'd been when she was outside, her body shaking with it.

"What was your marriage like?"

The question seemed to come out of left field, and Charlotte wasn't even certain she'd heard it right. "What?"

"Your marriage. Did Adam beat you?"

"Of course not."

"Mistreat you? Yell at you? Curse at you? Make you feel like you didn't matter?"

"He made me feel like the most important person in his life," she responded honestly. "We were best friends in middle school, a couple in high school. I thought…"

"That you'd be together forever?"

"I'm not sure what this has to do with anything, Wren," she responded, pulling the towel a little tighter around her shoulders. "Adam and I were kids when we married."

"Eighteen and nineteen," she responded. Obviously, she knew the story. She'd probably read whatever background report the FBI had done when Adam had gotten his security clearance.

"Right. Like I said. We were kids."

"You were legally adults. Me? I was sixteen."

"When you got married?" Charlotte glanced at Wren's ring finger, but there was no band on her left hand. No diamond. Not even a ring of pale flesh indicating that she ever wore them.

"Yes. Rafael was twenty-seven."

"And marrying him was legal?" She sounded shocked. She *was* shocked.

"My parents signed the papers. We were married by the pastor of our church. It was very common in our church community to marry young and to marry someone quite a bit older." She shrugged. "But that's another story for another time. Rafael and I were married for a long time. He never made me feel important."

"I'm sorry," Charlotte offered.

"I didn't tell you that part of my story to get your sympathy. I told you because you and Adam seemed to have had something special."

"*Had* is the correct word," Charlotte cut in.

"Maybe, but losing your son didn't mean you lost your love for your husband or that he lost his love for you. You went different directions, grieved in different ways, but none of that changed how you felt about one another."

It was a statement rather than a question, and she didn't wait for Charlotte to respond.

She stood, shrugging out of her coat and leaving it on the back of the chair. Her white button-up blouse was still crisp and wrinkle free, her shoulder holster snug against her lean frame. "I'm going to check the other doors and windows to make certain everything is locked. We'll keep the shades and curtains closed. If the dog needs to go out, let me know. I'll take him. Why don't you take a shower and warm up? Adam didn't save your life so you could freeze to death."

She walked into the hall, disappearing from view.

Charlotte could hear her footsteps on the floor and the brush of her slacks as she moved. She was probably walking into Charlotte's room, checking the window and pulling the curtains closed. She was probably also noticing the picture that still sat on the dresser. The one of Charlotte, Daniel and Adam on the first camping trip they'd taken as a family.

Daniel had been tiny. Just four months old, dressed in a blue onesie, his little legs dangling from a carrier strapped to Adam's chest. He'd been asleep. They'd been smiling. Behind them, a river had bounced over rocks, the water splashing into the air and creating a rainbow.

Maybe Charlotte should have put the photo away years ago, but she'd never been able to make herself. It was a snapshot of life before things had gotten hard, a photo of a young couple who'd had their entire lives ahead of them.

They'd had no clue what the future would bring.

They hadn't known about Daniel's autism. They hadn't experienced his head banging or screaming or self-harm behaviors. They hadn't spent hours and days and weeks and months in therapy with him, doing everything they could to find a way into his world.

They hadn't lost him.

Or themselves.

She blinked, hot tears pooling behind her eyes.

They were as surprising as the memory that she'd allowed to surface.

Tears weren't her thing.

Neither was dwelling on the past.

She walked into the bathroom, turning on the water and letting it heat up. She'd promised to stay in the cottage until Adam returned. She hadn't promised that she wouldn't go to the hospital after that.

She'd shower, change and wait.

When he returned, she'd get in her Jeep and go to the hospital. Doing that would be easier than sitting in the cottage remembering all the things that had once made her life so beautiful.

* * *

The logging camp had changed a lot in the years since Adam had last been there. Most of the shanties had collapsed. The ones that remained looked like they'd recently been used by campers and hikers, their support beams reinforced and their roofs thatched with layers of dry grass and mud. What had once been a clearing was now filled with sapling trees and sparse grass. Dead leaves and pine needles littered the ground and muffled his footsteps as he moved through the camp. He glanced across the clearing. River should be around, moving as silently as Adam as he searched for signs that a vehicle had been there.

It had to have been there.

They'd driven most of the length of the road, moving slowly and searching for breaks in the trees and foliage. There'd been no indication that the shooter had pulled off the road. River had stopped the Cadillac a couple of miles from the camp, and they'd walked in, splitting up when they reached a sign that had fallen years ago and was nothing but rusted, rotting metal.

The wind blew through the clearing, picking up debris and scattering it across the ground. If a truck had been there, the tracks had already been covered.

It had been there. It still must be.

If the shooter hadn't pulled over and hidden his vehicle, if he hadn't driven back to the main road, this was the only place left to go.

Leaves rustled and grass whispered, its hushed murmur familiar and comforting. As a kid, he'd spent more time outside than inside. He'd learned nature's sounds, and he preferred them to just about anything else.

The only thing better had been the sound of Daniel's giggles and the soft sigh of Charlotte's breath as she slept.

It was never quiet in Boston. Traffic was always busy, horns honking, people shouting, engines rumbling. Even in the darkest hours of the night, the noise drifted through his apartment window—a not-so-subtle reminder that he'd succeeded in accomplishing his goals and achieving his dreams. He'd applied and been accepted to the FBI. He'd moved from small-town America to the city. He'd bought a little apartment in a well-established neighborhood.

And yet, he felt like he'd failed, because he hadn't done any of it with Charlotte by his side.

He frowned, stepping around one of the old shanties that had been reroofed. The wind gusted, and he caught a whiff of dirt, dried grass and...soap?

He inhaled deeply, trying to figure out where the scent of soap was coming from. The shanty?

He crept around the old hut, moving as silently as he could. There was no door on the front of the structure. Just a rectangular hole where one used to be. He could have ducked a couple of inches and walked inside, but he couldn't see what was waiting for him there. He was certain something was. He could hear it scrabbling around in the darkness. Not a raccoon or possum. Whatever was in the shanty was much larger and heavier than either of those things.

A person?

That was what he suspected. He didn't pull his phone out or try to signal River. He didn't want to give away his presence. He'd been hunting the Night Stalker for three years. He was closer than he'd ever been to finding him. He could feel it the same way he felt the cold wind and the first icy drops of rain.

He rounded the shanty, eyeing a back door that hung listlessly from its frame. It banged against the exterior wall, thudding rhythmically with the gusting wind. He walked toward it, staying to the left of the opening and out of sight of anyone who might be inside.

This was the part of the job he loved most—the quick hit of adrenaline as he closed in on the criminal, the rush of energy that sharpened his thinking and his senses.

A figure appeared in the doorway, a black shape in the darkness, darting outside and racing for the edge of the clearing.

"FBI," Adam shouted, pulling his firearm but not discharging it. "Freeze!"

The person skidded to a stop a hundred yards away.

"Down on the ground," Adam commanded. "Keep your hands where I can see them."

"Don't shoot," a woman responded.

"Down on the ground," Adam repeated, moving toward the woman as she dropped onto her stomach, her arms splayed out beside her.

"I didn't do anything wrong," she said as he approached. "I just needed a place to stay."

"How long have you been out here?" he asked, flashing a light onto her prone figure. She was young. Probably not even out of her teens, her hair buzz-cut and dyed purple, a half dozen studs in the ear Adam could see.

"I don't know. Maybe a couple of days."

"It's not a good time of year to be living outside."

"I wasn't outside until you came around."

"There's no heat in that shack. It's a thatched roof and a storm is blowing in. You're going to be wet and cold by the time the night ends." He patted her down, pulling a bowie knife from the pocket of her cargo-style pants and a Swiss Army knife from her combat boot.

"I need those," she muttered, but she didn't make any effort to reach for them.

"What's your name?" he responded.

"Why do you want to know?"

"It might be a good idea just to give the answer," River said, stepping out of the shadows near the edge of the clearing. "You're on state land posted with no-trespassing signs. Squatting. That's never a good thing as far as the law is concerned."

"If you *are* the law," she said, scrambling to her feet.

She didn't run, but she looked like she wanted to—her muscles tense, her fists clenched.

"We are." Adam holstered his firearm and pulled out his wallet, flashing the badge he always carried.

"Whatever," she muttered, sounding exactly like the teenager she obviously was. "I'm not doing anything wrong."

"I think I mentioned trespassing," River responded, walking past her.

She winced, the movement so subtle Adam

wouldn't have noticed if he hadn't been watching so carefully. He'd seen other teenagers react that way when someone they didn't know got too close. All of them had been victims of violent crimes or abuse.

"I didn't see the signs," she claimed.

Adam didn't point out the white sign nearly glowing against a dark tree trunk a few feet away.

"Maybe not," River replied as he neared the threshold of the shanty's door. "But you were still doing it. Is anyone with you?"

"I'm standing here by myself, aren't I?"

"How about inside? Anyone in there?" River asked.

"No."

"You're sure about that?"

"Of course I am."

"I guess we're about to find out how honest you are," River said, pulling out his firearm and stepping into the darkness beyond the shanty's door.

"Hey!" the girl protested. "You can't just go into my place and look around. You need a search warrant."

"First, it's not your place," Adam responded, because River had already disappeared from sight. "It's state land. Second, if there's someone else in there, now is the time to say so."

"There's no one else," she huffed. "Just my stuff, and I don't want anyone touching it."

"He's not going to touch your things."

She snorted. "Like I'd believe anything you tell me."

"Is there a reason why you think I'd lie?"

She pressed her lips together and didn't speak.

"If you don't want to answer that question, how about we go back to the previous one. What's your name?"

She hesitated and then shrugged. "Savannah Johnson."

"Are you a runaway, Savannah?"

"I'm eighteen. I can go where I want and do what I want."

"*Were* you a runaway?" He rephrased the question, and she frowned.

"I'll take your silence as assent. Where did you run from?"

"Providence, Rhode Island. Can we be done now? I want to get my things and clear out before you decide to toss me in jail for trespassing."

"I'm not interested in throwing you in jail. I'm interested in getting some information from you."

"What information?" she asked, her expression guarded.

"A car drove into this area earlier. Did you see it?"

She hesitated, her gaze darting away. "I've been inside all night."

"You're avoiding my question again."

"I try to mind my own business."

"That's hard to do when it's the middle of the night in the middle of nowhere and someone drives through in a car."

"A truck," she corrected and then pressed her lips together.

"So, you did see the vehicle?"

"Are you going to let me leave if I answer your questions?"

"That depends on whether or not there are any outstanding warrants for your arrest."

"I'm not a criminal," she muttered.

"We'll still have to run your information before we release you."

"I'm not a criminal," she repeated. "And I did see the truck. It drove right through the middle of the clearing and headed that way." She gestured toward an abandoned road that had been used to transport logs to barges that would carry them across the lake to the trains that had once run endless shipments of lumber up and down the east coast.

"Did you see anything else?"

"No, I was packing my stuff and getting ready to hit the road when I heard you coming."

"Packing up? Why?"

"I heard a gunshot before the truck drove through. Up until tonight, things have been quiet here. Now they aren't." She shrugged. "I don't like taking chances."

He didn't, either. And right now, he felt like they were. The lake was only a half mile from the logging camp. A quick walk even at night. The Night Stalker could be standing feet away, watching from the trees. Or he could be hiking back to the cottage, hoping for another shot at Charlotte.

"All clear in there," River said, rounding the side of the shanty and striding toward them. "I texted Wren. Honor arrived. She's on the way here to collect our—" he glanced at Savannah and said "—witness."

"I'm not a witness," she protested, a hint of panic and fear in her voice.

She was a kid, and she was scared.

In other circumstances, Adam would have taken the time to reassure her. Right now, he wanted to find the truck that she'd seen.

"You want to wait for her here?" he asked River. "I'll head down to the lake."

"You're on leave, remember?"

"I think my leave ended around the time a

bullet slammed into the ground a few inches from my head. Since I know the area better than you, I'll head to the lake." He was already striding across the clearing.

River didn't try to stop him.

Like Adam, he knew just how close they were getting, just how precious every second was. Finding the truck would be great, but they were seeking a bigger prize.

The Night Stalker had already ended the lives of people who had hopes, dreams and aspirations. He'd stolen the futures of women who had spent their lives serving and helping others. He'd left empty spots at dinner tables, giant holes in hearts.

If he wasn't caught, he'd continue.

And his next victim would be Charlotte.

Adam found the old road and stepped into the foliage beside it, moving quietly as he navigated the terrain. Drops of rain turned into a downpour that soaked his hair and slid down the collar of his coat. He ignored it. His focus was on the glint of lake water he could see through the trees. The truck had to be parked on the beach. If the Night Stalker knew the area, he'd know he'd hit the end of the road. That there was nowhere to go but back. He'd have two choices. Stay with the vehicle or leave it.

Adam knew he'd leave. The killer was smart and cunning. He weighed odds before he took risks. Sitting around in a truck hoping he wouldn't be discovered was the kind of chance he wouldn't take.

The question was, what direction had he gone?

Back toward Charlotte or away?

The truck was the place to begin the hunt.

Adam stepped out of the trees and into winter-dry marsh grass, scanning the rock-strewn beach littered with rotting logs. An old dock protruded into the lake. Sturdily built to hold the weight of trucks and their lumber loads, it had weathered the test of time. Near the end of it, so close to the lake a strong push would have sent it tumbling in, a truck sat abandoned, its headlights on, its driver's door open.

Adam pulled his firearm, his body humming with adrenaline as he probed the darkness and tried to find some sign that the Night Stalker was still there.

Rain fell in sheets, masking sounds and reducing visibility, but the beach looked and felt empty. He eyed the truck, the headlights, the door, the lake beyond the dock. At first, he saw nothing. Then a dark shape separated itself from the rain-speckled surface of the lake.

He watched as it glided across the water. A boat. It had to be. No motor. It wasn't speeding away; it was moving languidly as if the person steering it had all the time in the world.

Adam raced across the beach, pounding onto the dock, his gaze focused on the boat. He could see the person in it now—a hunched figure paddling toward the distant shore.

The Night Stalker.

His flesh crawled with the knowledge.

He tried to make out details, but rain and distance obscured his view. He wouldn't be able to add anything to the description Charlotte had provided. He wasn't close enough to fire a shot, either.

He grabbed his phone and dialed Wren's number.

They needed manpower on the other side of the lake and they needed a boat, because Adam wasn't going to stand on a dock watching as a cold-blooded murderer made his escape.

FIVE

The Night Stalker was out on the lake.

Charlotte doubted she was supposed to know that. She'd been pacing her room, trying not to think about Adam out in the rain hunting a killer, trying not to imagine what would happen if he came face-to-face with the Night Stalker. Wren had been in the living room, setting up equipment that a pretty blonde agent named Honor had brought. She'd had no idea how thin the walls were or how easily sound traveled through closed cottage doors. Charlotte hadn't been trying to listen to the conversation, but she'd heard enough of it to understand what was going on. Adam and River had found the truck, and they'd spotted the gunman fleeing in a rowboat. The local authorities had been called and a Whisper Lake police boat was being readied.

She'd been hearing sirens for ten minutes, and she knew state and local law enforcement had responded. They were creating a drag-net to bring the Night Stalker in, and she was pacing her room, praying that they'd be suc-cessful.

She wanted her life back before she for-got how little it resembled the life she'd once dreamed she'd have. When she was a kid, she'd thought she'd grow up and be like her mother—a modern-day nomad who didn't want to set down roots.

Even after she'd moved in with her grand-parents and experienced small-town life, she'd been certain that one day she'd travel the world. She'd never pictured herself married with children. She hadn't wanted the white picket fence and the cute house and the puppy.

Until she and Adam had fallen from friend-ship to love. *Then* those dreams had formed.

Even more, she'd finally understood that home was always and only in the hearts of the people she loved. Location had stopped mat-tering. Traveling had ceased to be her goal. She'd been willing to stay in Whisper Lake or move to a big city or buy a tract home in the suburbs. She'd known she could be happy and content anywhere her little family was.

And then her family was gone, her heart shattered, everything she'd believed about the path her life had taken changed. She'd re-created her dreams; she'd refocused her energy. She'd convinced herself that this life was the one she wanted.

One look in Adam's eyes had changed that.

One look in his face had reminded her that an empty cottage on the lake couldn't take the place of scrawny-armed hugs from her little boy or late-night talks with the only man she'd ever loved.

A hot tear rolled down her cheek, and she brushed it away impatiently. She wasn't going to go backward. She wasn't going to waste one more second of her time hoping and praying that Adam would come back to her. She'd given that fantasy up the day she'd signed the divorce papers. Even if she hadn't, they were different people now. They'd grown up and matured and moved on.

"And it will do you a lot of good to remember it," she muttered.

Clover whined, and she dropped down beside him, pulling his sturdy body close. "It's just you and me, Clover. And I'm perfectly fine with that."

Clover whined again, dropping his head onto her thigh and staring into her eyes. He probably wanted a late-night walk, but she'd promised she'd stay inside. She wouldn't break that promise, but she was going to be very sure not to make any more.

Someone knocked on the door, and she jumped, swiping her hand down her cheek to make sure all the moisture was gone.

"Come in," she called, and the door opened.

She was expecting Wren or Honor.

She wasn't expecting Adam, but he was there, his hair wet from the rain, a few drops of moisture sliding down his neck.

She wanted to wipe them away.

She wanted to grab a towel from the linen closet and dry his hair, tug off his sopping-wet coat and wrap him in a comforter. She wanted to do a dozen things that she had no right to, so she stood and shoved her hands into the pockets of the oversize cardigan she wore.

"Did you find him?" she asked, and he shook his head.

"Not yet. We had a visual, but the rain picked up, and we lost it. The Whisper Lake police just dropped a boat in the water. Hopefully, they'll be able to find him before he goes to shore."

"What if they don't?"

"Then we'll keep looking. He left his truck on that old loading dock down near the logging camp. We've got a team collecting evidence there. I plan to rejoin them shortly, but I wanted to check on you."

"You didn't have to."

"Yes. I did," he said simply. No extra words or embellishments. Just the facts. Just like always, and it reminded her of the teenager she'd met her first day at Whisper Lake Middle School, of the young man she'd married, of the grief-stricken parent she'd let walk away.

"Adam, this isn't a good idea," she said. She was staring into his eyes, seeing the man she'd loved with all her heart, the one she'd planned to spend the rest of her life with, and she couldn't help wondering what would have happened if she'd followed him out the door five and a half years ago, if she'd walked him to his car. If she'd begged him to stay.

"What?" he asked. "Me making sure you stay safe? Because if that's what you're talking about, then it's not just a good idea. It's a great one."

"You being part of my life again," she corrected. "Even if it's just for a few days or weeks. Even if it's only because there's a killer after me."

"I guess you have a reason for saying that," he commented. "Because from where I'm standing, I can't see one good reason to walk away when you need my help."

"I've got local, state and federal police helping me. That makes your presence a little redundant," she pointed out.

"I'm a federal police officer, so that point is moot. What's the real reason you don't want me around, Charlotte? Because I know there is one."

"Having you around just feels too..." *Right*. That was what she wanted to say, but she couldn't. Not without giving him a glimpse into the most vulnerable part of her soul.

"It feels what?" he prodded, and she swallowed down the truth, reached for the word she thought she should say, the one that was guaranteed to keep distance between them.

"Wrong," she managed, and he frowned.

"That's not the word I would put to it," he said, his tone curt and a little hard.

"You asked *me* to put a word to it, Adam," she reminded him. "I did. Let's not spend time arguing over whose perspective is more valid."

"No argument. I was just making a statement. If you feel that way, I'll respect it." He stared into her eyes as he spoke, and she was certain he knew she'd been lying, that what she felt was vastly different than what she'd said.

She could have told him the truth.

She could have allowed herself to be that vulnerable.

But she'd been hurt before, and she didn't ever want to be hurt again. Not by anyone, but especially not by Adam.

"Have you heard from the hospital?" she asked, changing the subject. "I've been worried sick about Bubbles." *And you.* If she'd been braver, she'd have added that. Not because he elicited such strong feelings in her and she wanted him to know it, but because they'd shared a past and caring about him without loving him should have been possible.

"We've got an agent there making sure she stays safe. He called Wren a few minutes ago. Bubbles is awake and lucid."

"Thank the Lord," she whispered, and he nodded.

"A few more minutes in the water and the outcome wouldn't have been as good."

"Does she remember what happened? How she fell in the lake?"

"No. She stopped by here to let Clover out before she went to bed. When she opened the door to leave, he started barking and darted out the door. She thought you were home, so she stepped outside to say hello. Only, of course, you weren't there."

"Did she see whoever was?"

"She didn't see anything. Clover had run toward the road, and she was worried about him. She headed that way. Her memories are blank after that. The doctor seems pretty confident they'll return eventually. For now, it's probably best that she doesn't remember. When she arrived at the ER, there were bruises on her forearms and her neck that looked like finger marks. She also had a head injury. The doctor can't say how that happened, but it was likely caused by blunt force trauma. For a woman Bubbles's age, not remembering might be best."

"Poor Bubbles," she murmured. "I really wish I could be there with her."

"I'll take you after I finish here."

"Really?"

"Have I ever lied to you?"

"Only when you said you'd love me forever," she responded, the words popping out unbidden.

He stilled, his eyes drilling into hers, a million words suddenly dancing in the air between them.

"Who said I ever stopped loving you?" he finally asked, his voice gentle and filled with things that she was better off not acknowledging.

"This probably isn't the time to have this conversation," she responded, her throat dry, her heart pounding. She wanted to reach for him, to slide her arms around his waist like she had hundreds of times before. To rest her head against his chest and listen to the strong steady beat of his heart.

"We didn't find the Night Stalker at the logging camp, but we did find someone else," he said, his tone clipped and businesslike, all the warmth and gentleness gone.

He'd shown her a piece of his heart.

She'd shown him nothing but fear.

She already regretted that, but he'd turned away and was stepping back into the hall. Any chance she had of making it right had been gone the minute she'd made it wrong. Just like before, she'd let him go. Only this time her grief over Daniel's death wasn't as raw, her sorrow wasn't a deep well that she was drowning in. Her mind was clearer, her thoughts more focused, and she knew in her heart she was making another mistake.

"Adam," she said, following him out of the room, ready to tell him the truth—that she'd never stopped loving him, either.

He kept walking, and she could feel the old broken places in her heart, the places that she'd slowly knit back together after he'd left, coming apart again.

She cleared her throat, told herself she wasn't going to cry.

"Who did you find at the logging camp?" she managed to ask.

"A runaway. She's in the living room. She'll be staying here until Wren decides how much she saw and whether or not she's going to be a federal witness." His tone had changed completely. He sounded…unfazed and unaffected.

"What's her name?" she asked, striving to sound exactly the same.

"Savannah Johnson," he responded as he walked into the living room. She followed, saw a young girl sitting on the couch. Stiff, tense, scared. That was how she looked, her hair buzz-cut and purple, studs in both ears and one in her left eyebrow. A military-green T-shirt clung to her skinny frame, and cargo-style camouflage pants bagged around her lean legs. A dark jacket lay beside her on the couch, and a duffel bag sat at her combat-booted feet. Tough clothes, tough haircut, but nothing could change the sweetness of her face. She had pale skin and freckles and a delicate bone structure that made her look like a middle school kid.

"Hello," Charlotte said, walking across the room and offering her hand. "I'm Charlotte Murray."

"Savannah." Her grip was confident, but her hand was freezing, her fingers icy. "Sorry to bust in on you like this. They wouldn't let me leave."

"I don't mind. Clover and I like company."

"Clover?"

"My dog." She didn't have to call him. He'd already padded down the hall.

Savannah's eyes widened as he nudged his head into Charlotte's hand and leaned against her leg.

"This," Charlotte said, patting his curly side, "is Clover."

"Are you sure he's a dog? He looks more like a miniature bear," Savannah said, but she was smiling, her expression soft.

"He's a dog, and he loves to be petted. He also loves sitting on that couch with our guests and pretending that I never give him any attention. Do you mind if he joins you?"

"No." Savannah shifted to the side, one pant leg riding up and revealing a skinny shin pockmarked with what looked like old cigarette burns.

"Place," Charlotte commanded Clover, her gaze shifting to Adam.

He'd seen the marks. She could see it in the tightness of his jaw, the anger in his eyes.

Clover jumped onto the couch and dropped his big head onto Savannah's lap, looking up at her adoringly. He was an exceptional therapy dog, in tune with the emotions of the people he visited. He sensed something in Savannah that made him cuddle close and lie still.

She touched his head tentatively, a soft smile curving the corners of her mouth.

"Hello, Clover," she murmured.

His tail thumped, and he looked at Charlotte. She gave him the signal to stay.

"I'm going to make some hot chocolate," she announced.

Savannah stopped petting Clover and scowled.

"I'm not two," she said.

"Did I say it was for you?" Charlotte responded. She'd been Savannah's age once. She'd had the big attitude, the chip on the shoulder and the need to be in control. She hadn't had physical scars, but she'd had plenty of emotional ones.

"No, but—"

"This kind of weather demands warmth and sugar. Besides, I'm more of a hot chocolate drinker than a coffee drinker," she cut in. "I'm going to have some. With whipped cream. If you'd rather have coffee, I can make that, too."

"Either is fine," Savannah said grudgingly, her hand back on Clover's head.

"Cool. It should only take a couple of minutes." She walked away, snagging Adam's wrist as she went.

The open floor plan didn't offer much in the way of privacy, so she dragged him through the kitchen, past the table where Wren sat staring at a computer monitor and into the mudroom.

"We're not going outside," Adam said, stopping short a few feet from the door.

Her fingers were still curved around his wrist, and she knew she should release her hold, but she held on as she leaned close and whispered, "Where did she come from?"

"She was squatting in a shanty in the logging camp. She saw the truck but not enough details to be helpful. We're keeping her here while we check her story, make sure she's really eighteen and that she doesn't have a warrant out for her arrest."

"Eighteen? She looks twelve!"

"She has ID that says otherwise. A driver's license and a copy of her birth certificate and social security card."

"She's well prepared for her age, isn't she?" She glanced into the kitchen. Wren was still hunched over the table and the screen.

"You saw the scars, Charlotte. She probably had to be to protect herself," he said.

"Where's she from? How did she get here? She sure isn't from Whisper Lake. I'd have recognized the purple hair and eyebrow studs."

"If her story is to be believed, Rhode Island. She claims she ran away. Since she's eighteen, she can do what she wants as long as she's not breaking any laws."

"Trespassing on private property is against the law."

"Do you really think the Whisper Lake Sheriff's Department is going to press charges for that? She's a kid. She was looking for shelter from the elements."

"Of course not, and they shouldn't. I was just pointing out that she wasn't exactly abiding by the law. Not that it matters. She could freeze to death out there. We have at least another month of winter temperatures before it starts warming up."

"That's why I brought her here instead of having the local police take her to the station. I was afraid her story would check out, and they'd release her. She'd be out on her own again. Most stories that begin that way don't end well." He glanced at his watch. "I need to go back to the camp. Your promise stands, right? You're not leaving the house until I return."

"You already returned," she pointed out, finally finding the strength to release his wrist.

He caught her hand before she could move away, and just like every time he touched her, she felt his warmth seeping into her blood, pulsing into her heart, pulling her back to those very first days when they'd laughed at each other's middle school jokes and helped each other with homework.

She'd loved him even then.

He'd made her feel valuable and funny and smart.

Those were things she'd never felt in her parents' home. She'd been the afterthought, the kid who got in the way of them doing their own things. How many times had her mother screamed that Charlotte was the biggest mistake she'd ever made? How many mornings had her father told her to go back to her room so that he could eat in peace?

Her grandparents had been wonderful warm human beings, but by the time Charlotte had been shipped off to live with them, she'd already learned that she had minimal value, that what she wanted didn't matter and that she was more trouble than she was worth.

Adam had never seen her that way, and after a while, she'd begun to view herself through his eyes. She'd started to see her innate value and understand her worth in a way she never could have without his friendship.

"Don't split hairs, Charlotte," Adam said, his voice gruffer and deeper than it had been when they were married. "You made the promise. I'm holding you to it. If I'm out there worrying about you, I'm not going to be as effective or focused as I need to be."

"I'm not your worry, Adam," she said, and she meant it. She'd learned to go it alone. Having him suddenly appear back in her life wasn't going to change the person she'd become in the years since he'd left. It certainly wasn't going to make her start needing him again.

But there was a part of her that wanted it to. There was that space in her heart that he'd once filled, that secret spot that had stayed empty since the day he'd walked away.

She shuddered, rubbing her arms to try to ease the chill.

He watched dispassionately, whatever he was feeling hidden in the depths of his dark gray eyes. When he finally spoke, he sounded as weary as she felt. "Now isn't the time to discuss it, so how about we just agree that you're a witness to a crime that the FBI is investigating. You're the victim of a serial killer we're hunting. The best and only thing that you should be doing is staying close to the people who can protect you."

He opened the back door and walked outside, leaving before she could argue. That was for the best. She had no reasonable argument to make. Until the Night Stalker was apprehended, going to the hospital without a law enforcement escort would be as foolish as climbing Mount Everest without an oxygen tank. She could attempt it, but the likelihood of coming out alive was slim to none.

She'd wait and go when he returned, because it was the intelligent thing to do. She'd follow the rules the FBI set for her because she valued the life God had given her. It wasn't what she'd expected. It wasn't what she'd wanted. It wasn't anything she ever could have imagined when she'd promised to love Adam forever, but it was a good life. It was one that she'd created out of the ashes of the old, and there was a lot of beauty in that.

The old boards in the kitchen creaked and Wren appeared in the doorway, her dark eyes trained on Charlotte. She was an FBI agent who headed an elite team. There was no doubt that she was accomplished and successful. She had a past, though, that sounded a lot different than her present. She'd hinted at it—married at sixteen to a man in his twenties, raised in a church that encouraged that, parents who saw nothing wrong with letting their sixteen-year-old child wed.

If Charlotte had known Wren better, she'd

have asked how that had come about and how it had ended.

She didn't, so she smiled and walked into the kitchen. "I'm making hot chocolate. Want some?"

"I've already had enough coffee to keep me awake for a month. I think I'll skip the extra caffeine."

"I have decaffeinated coffee," she offered, reaching into the pantry closet and pulling out the ingredients she needed for the hot chocolate.

"I'm fine. Thanks."

Charlotte nodded but didn't speak again. Her throat was thick with what felt suspiciously like tears. That was odd, because she almost never cried.

She poured milk and cream into a pot, added chocolate nibs and a scoop of sugar and then set it on the burner. Her back was to the sink and the window that looked out into the yard. She knew the curtains were closed and that no one could see her, but she felt exposed and vulnerable. She turned on the gas burner, her hands shaking, her heart beating hollowly in her chest. The brownish liquid splashed out of the pot as she clumsily stirred it.

"Let me." Wren nudged her aside and took the spoon from her hand.

"I can manage."

"Not without making a colossal mess."

"It's my kitchen. It will be my mess, so I guess that doesn't matter."

"Sure it does. Who wants a mess to clean up? Not me or you. Besides," she added, glancing toward the living room. Savannah and Clover were still on the couch, both of them relaxed and content. "Your time would be better spent with her."

"My time?"

"She needs someone to talk to," Wren said quietly. "Aside from basic information, she's refused to tell anyone on my team anything. Maybe you can get her to open up."

"About what she saw tonight?"

"About why she ran away and how she ended up here," Wren corrected. "She's been through something, and I want to know what."

"I don't know that she'll be any more willing to open up to me than she was to you," Charlotte hedged, her gaze on Savannah. They were speaking so softly it would be nearly impossible for the teenager to hear, but she'd tensed, her hands dropping away from Clover.

"I'd appreciate it if you at least gave it a try," Wren responded. "My team isn't just about the cases we're working. It's about helping people who can't help themselves and seeking justice for those who don't have the power to do so on their own. Something happened to that kid. I want to know what and when and how she escaped, and then I want to make whoever hurt her pay."

She said it without emotion, but Charlotte could see rage simmering in her eyes.

"I'll try," she said.

"Thank you. While you do that, I'll add a little more chocolate to our treat." She grabbed the container of nibs and dumped another handful to the pot."

"I thought you said you weren't having any."

"That was when I thought you were going to tear open one of those awful packets, pour its contents into a mug and add some hot water."

"You're a hot chocolate snob?"

"I'm a lot of things, but first and foremost, I'm an FBI agent. Go on in the living room. I want you to stay as far away from the windows and doors as possible."

"Everything is closed up tight."

"That won't mean a whole lot if the Night Stalker decides to empty a round into the front of the house."

"You have security cameras all over the exterior," Charlotte pointed out. "It would be really hard for him to get close enough to do that."

Wren snorted. "How close did he need to be to nearly take you out while we were down at the beach?"

"Not very close."

"Exactly. Security cameras see what is in front of them. I set up a few at the perimeter of the yard, but if he knows this area—and it's pretty obvious that he does—he'll be able to find another vantage point to shoot from."

"If he does that, all of us will be in danger."

"Yeah. That's a good argument for going to a safe house, isn't it? Since we're here for now, the best thing you can do is stay in the center of the house. Go on." She gestured toward the living room. "I'll have this done in no time."

Charlotte went, because she'd told herself she'd play by the FBI's rules and because she was as curious about Savannah as Wren was.

Someone had put those marks on the teenager. Someone had been the reason she'd left Rhode Island and traveled to Maine. Someone really did need to pay for hurting the young girl.

Trying to find out who was responsible seemed like a lot better use of Charlotte's time than sitting in her room thinking about the past, worrying about the present and wondering about the future. If the by-product of focusing on Savannah meant getting her mind off Adam, that would be a bonus.

She walked into the living room, settled into the old recliner and met Savannah's eyes. "You and Clover seem to be getting along well."

"He's a sweet dog."

"Did you have a dog before you…" Her voice trailed off, because she wasn't sure what Savannah called it. Running away? Escaping? Making a new life for herself?

"Ran away? No. I was in foster care. Nothing in any of those houses was mine."

"Houses? How many placements did you have?"

"A lot." She gently nudged Clover off her lap and stood. "And I'm not going to discuss them with you or Agent Santino or a shrink, okay? If the feds want my information, they can subpoena Providence County for it. I'm sure family services will be happy to provide them with a copy of all my records."

"Savannah, we just want to help you," she said calmly, knowing that the words wouldn't matter, that nothing she said to the teenager would make a difference.

"Help me help you, right? Your buddies want to find the guy who was driving that truck, right? They think he's some sort of se- rial killer."

"He is a serial killer," Wren called from the kitchen.

"Yeah. Well, that has nothing to do with me, but I can tell you this—if you want the right information, you have to ask the right questions."

"What do you mean?" Charlotte asked.

"Everyone has asked me what I saw tonight. They all want to know about the truck and the guy who was driving it. No one bothered asking if he'd ever been in the camp before. I mean, I made it pretty clear that I'd been staying there for a few days. I'd think people would want to know if that was the first time I saw him."

"Was it?" she asked, surprised by the ve- hemence in Savannah's tone.

"No. He drove through there last night and the night before. Both times, he went down to the beach. I don't know what he was doing the first time, but the second time he dropped off a boat."

"How do you know this?" Wren stepped into the room, her dark eyes flashing with interest.

"I may be young, but I'm not stupid. I've been in that camp for eight days—"

"That's way more than the few days you told us about," Wren interrupted, and Savannah shrugged.

"So? Who does it matter to? It's not like I have anyone waiting for me at home. It's not like I even have a home," Savannah replied.

Her words were like daggers to Charlotte's heart.

Wren didn't seem quite as affected.

She strode to the kitchen table and grabbed a notebook and pen. "You'd been there for eight days, and he hadn't been there before? Is that what you're saying?" she asked.

"What I'm saying is that I hadn't seen or heard anyone the entire time I was in that shack. Then he started coming. He came the first night, drove down to the beach and stayed a few minutes. The next night, he came again and was at the beach even longer. I think it was probably two hours, but I don't have a watch, so I'm not sure."

"Two hours is a long time," Charlotte said. "Were you worried that he was going to find you?"

"I barely breathed the whole time. I even told myself I was going to leave the next day, but that shack was a lot nicer than any shelter I'd been in. I had a bed and some food, and I didn't have to worry that…" She shook her head. "Anyway, I told myself I was going to leave, but first I wanted to see if I could figure out what he'd been doing down at the dock."

"Did you?" Wren asked, taking a seat next to Savannah, still writing in her notebook.

"Well, I found the boat. He'd tied it to the dock and left it there."

"Anything in it?"

Savannah hesitated.

"Hon," Wren said with a sigh. "There is no way you saw that boat tied there and didn't look through its contents. Charlotte and I would have done exactly the same. Right?" She glanced at Charlotte.

"I know *I* would have," she responded. "I mean, the guy was down there for something, and I'd have been assuming it wasn't a fishing trip. It's not fishing season, and it's too cold to be out on the water for very long."

"He wasn't fishing," Savannah said. "And the boat wasn't big enough to hold much. It was a canoe. One of those plastic-looking ones. There was storage space under the seats, and he had some canned food, electrical tape, some women's clothes. Rope. Fire starts. A knife. And a locked box I couldn't get into."

"You tried?" Charlotte asked.

"I thought there might be money in it. I wouldn't have taken much. Just enough to get me to a warmer state." She blushed, her hand dropping to Clover's head. "I'm not a thief," she added softly.

"It's obvious that you aren't," Wren replied. "You're a very smart and resourceful young woman. You are also very observant. The FBI often gives rewards for information leading to the arrest of criminals they've been searching for."

"I've heard of that," Savannah said.

"Have you? Then you won't be surprised when I tell you that you have two thousand dollars coming your way."

"I do?"

"You do. It will take a little time to process the funds, but I'll make sure you get them."

"Two thousand dollars?" Savannah repeated as if she couldn't believe the amount or her good fortune.

"Yes. Now, how about you go take advantage of being here. I'm sure Charlotte won't mind if you take a hot shower and put on some fresh clothes."

"I wouldn't mind at all," Charlotte agreed. "The linen closet is right outside the bathroom. I've got different soaps and lotions and shampoos. You can use whatever you want."

"Are you sure?" Savannah asked, but she

was already standing, nearly running into the hall.

"First door to the right," Charlotte called.

Seconds later, a door closed, and the sound of water rushing through the pipes filled the house.

"Well," Wren said, standing and brushing lint from her slacks. "That didn't take much convincing. I'd better go stir that chocolate."

"There isn't a two-thousand-dollar reward, is there?" Charlotte asked as Wren walked away.

"I never said that's what it was. I just said she had it coming to her."

"From where?"

"Me."

"That's a lot of cash to give to a kid you don't even know."

"I know her. She's me at that age. Only, I was married and wore pounds of makeup to hide the bruises. I need to make a few phone calls. The contents of the boat made me think the Night Stalker had some big plans."

She didn't say what those plans were.

Charlotte didn't ask.

It didn't take a rocket scientist to realize that all the things Savannah had listed were items a serial killer might use when he kidnapped his victim. From there, it was an easy jump to concluding that Charlotte had been the one he'd intended to grab.

He'd just needed an opportunity.

She'd almost given it to him.

If it hadn't been for Adam, she'd have returned home alone. She'd have gone to bed thinking she was safe, and she'd have woken to a nightmare.

SIX

There weren't a lot of things that scared Adam. He'd spent most of his childhood living in chaos, neglected by his mother, abused by her boyfriends, fending for himself because there'd been no one else. He could remember getting off the elementary school bus, shuffling along the dirt path that led to the front door of the single-wide trailer they lived in, wondering if there'd be food or lights or heat.

He knew what it was like to be hungry.

He knew what it was like to be cold in the winter and swelteringly hot in the summer.

He knew how to face down the toughest bully and how to take down a drunk man three times his size.

More than anything, he knew how to survive, how to fight, how to react quickly during crises. He had a dangerous job, but he didn't carry worry around as his companions. He focused his attention and energy on finding solutions to problems. He prayed, he trusted and he entered every situation knowing that God was in control.

Because of that, he was never consumed by fear.

Or, at least, he'd never been until now.

Now he was terrified.

Wren had called and offered information about what the Night Stalker had in his boat. If Savannah were to be believed, he had many of the tools that had been used to abduct and restrain previous victims. Each of the women who'd been found had had electric tape wrapped around her wrists and her ankles. Each had rope burns on her abdomen, healing cuts on her thighs and neck. The Night Stalker didn't just kidnap and kill his victims. He tortured them.

Adam had seen the autopsy reports, and he'd burned with rage for what the victims had suffered. Now the killer had Charlotte in his crosshairs, and the thought of her being abducted, tortured and killed left him cold with terror.

He frowned, watching as the Night Stalker's vehicle was lifted onto the truck that would bring it to the impound garage at Boston headquarters. The truck had already been picked clean of evidence, fingerprints obtained, DNA swabs taken from a spot of what looked like blood in the truck cab. Carpet had been pulled up from there, too, the fibers of it similar in color to ones that had been found on several of the Night Stalker's victims.

"What do you think?" Honor Remington asked. She'd dropped the security equipment off with Wren and then returned to take part in the investigation. "Is he still hanging around?"

"Yes," he responded without hesitation.

"I suppose you have good reasons for thinking that."

"This is his home base." Speaking the words out loud made him sick, but he'd been over the timeline of events dozens of times. He'd thought through every angle of the newest case, and there was no other reasonable explanation for how intimately the Night Stalker knew the area.

"That's what I thought you'd say. Kind of odd that he'd suddenly choose a victim so close to home. Up until now, he's kept his distance, right?" she asked, tucking a strand of blond hair back into the tight bun it had escaped. The newest member of the team, she was also the youngest and the least experienced. What she lacked in that area, she made up for in brains and work ethic. Adam didn't know anyone who worked harder than Honor.

"Right."

"I guess if we figure out why he changed his MO, we might be able to figure out who he is."

"You're guessing right. Of course, it would be easier if the plates on that truck would lead us to him. Then all we'd have to do was run them, and we'd have our name."

She snorted. "Right. Like he'd use plates that could be traced back to him."

"He didn't," River said, striding toward them. He had a flashlight in one hand and his phone in the other. "The plate was taken off a Buick owned by a guy in the next town over. He reported it missing a year ago. I gave him a call. He's not sure how long the tag was actually missing. He's the head maintenance worker at—" he glanced down at his phone "—Pine Valley Residential and Memory Care Center. They provide him with room, board and a truck to run errands. The Buick has been in the garage there since he took the job."

"I know the facility," Adam said. Charlotte's grandfather Robert had spent the last two years of his life there. Diagnosed with Alzheimer's at seventy, he'd remained at the cottage until Charlotte's grandmother Mildred had been unable to care for him any longer. Adam and Charlotte had been newlyweds when the decision was made to move him. He'd helped load Robert's things onto a truck and also unload them at the center. In the two years that followed, he and Charlotte had visited the facility several times a week every week. "What's the name of the guy who reported the plates missing?"

"Conrad O'Reilly." He glanced at his phone again. "Twenty-nine. High school graduate. Three speeding tickets in the past year, but no criminal record. I already scheduled an interview with him. He's out of town until Monday. I'm meeting him at nine in the morning on Tuesday."

"Out of town where?"

"Portland. His great-uncle died, and he's attending the funeral."

"Have you verified that?" Adam asked.

"In the ten minutes since I was given the information? No?" River responded. There was no mistaking the edge of sarcasm in his voice. He knew his job. He didn't need to be reminded of the proper way to do it.

"Right. Sorry. This whole thing has got me

on edge," Adam admitted. "The Night Stalker is a little too close to home."

"I thought home was in Boston," Honor said.

"Figure of speech. This is where I grew up. I know the town and the people and the way life works here."

"And you thought that because it was a small town with nice people in it, a serial killer couldn't emerge from its folds?" River tucked his phone away.

"You know that's not the case, River. I've seen all kinds of trouble coming from all kinds of places. I just mean that he's too close to people I care about. I've seen what he can do. I've studied what he's done. I've talked to the families of his victims, and I know exactly what the world lost when he snuffed out the lives of the women he killed. I want to find him. I want to throw him in prison, and I don't want him to ever have a chance to come out."

"We're on the same page, then. This guy has been on the loose for too long. He's hurt too many people." He sighed. "In the profile you wrote up, you mentioned that he probably had a job that allowed him to travel."

"That's right."

"Probably something in the medical field."

"Also correct."

"It seems to me that O'Reilly comes close to that."

"If working as a maintenance person at a memory care center counts as being in a medical field, I guess you're right." But it was a stretch. Especially because Adam's profile also suggested that the killer was a college graduate, a high-level professional, someone with disposable income that would allow him the financial freedom most people never obtained.

"I want to check his work history, find out just how much time he's taken off the past few years," River continued. "Maybe we can take a ride out there tomorrow. Before he returns."

"I hope you're not thinking of gathering information without getting the proper warrants," Honor said. "The last thing any of us want is to find evidence and then have it be inadmissible in court."

"I'll get the proper warrants," River assured her. "Once we catch this guy, he's not going free on a technicality. Looks like they're heading out." He pointed to the tow truck that was slowly making its way back across the dock.

"We're done here." Adam turned away, anxious to return to the cottage.

Anxious to return to Charlotte.

He could admit that to himself.

He refused to think about what it meant, though.

She'd made her feelings clear: she didn't want him in her life.

He didn't blame her. He'd walked away when she'd needed him most. He'd had a dozen excuses for it. He'd justified it in a hundred different ways, but the more time had passed, the more he'd realized the truth. He'd left because he hadn't been able to handle watching her mourn. There'd been nothing he could offer her. No comfort. No words that would make the nightmare go away.

His own heartbreak had nearly destroyed him, but watching Charlotte pick at her food, listening to her cry at night, looking on as her skin paled and her body grew frail, had made him feel helpless.

He'd hated that feeling, and he'd run from it, not her.

He should have explained it to her a long time ago.

Instead, he'd moved on, created a new life, achieved all the goals and dreams he'd once shared with Charlotte. But she hadn't been there to cheer him on, and the victories had seemed as hollow as the place in his soul that had once been filled with Daniel's giggles and Charlotte's laughter.

He pushed the thought away, forcing himself to focus on the case. If it were a puzzle, they were ready to place the last piece. Only it was missing, fallen in the crack of the heating vent or between old warped floorboards. Eventually, they'd track it down. Hopefully before someone else was hurt.

He passed the old shack where Savannah had been staying. He'd already walked through it, searching for any evidence that she hadn't spent her time there alone. He believed the Night Stalker was a lone wolf, a hunter who preferred his solitary pursuit, but there had been cases where a serial killer had solicited help from others. It was rare, but not unheard of, and Adam had to consider the possibility that Savannah wasn't as innocent as she was pretending to be.

His cell phone rang, and he answered without glancing at the caller ID. "Whitfield here," he said.

There was a quiet gasp of air, and then silence.

"Hello?" he prodded, glancing at the screen. The number wasn't one in his contact list.

"Adam?" a shaky female voice said. "Is that you?"

"Yes. Who's calling?"

"Bubbles Raymond. Your old neighbor," she said as if they hadn't seen each other several times in the days since he'd arrived in town.

"Is everything okay, Bubbles?"

"Well, no, it isn't. There's a man in my hospital room, and he refuses to leave."

"A man?"

"Yes. He says he's a coworker of yours. His name is Shane." A masculine voice rumbled in the background, and she sighed. "Sam. That's his name."

"He is my coworker, Bubbles. Didn't he show you his ID?"

"He did, but I thought it might be fake." She lowered her voice to a loud whisper. "He looks shifty."

"Shifty, huh?" he said, biting back laughter. Sam was a lot of things, but shifty wasn't one of them. He wore suits, ties and polished shoes. Kept his hair trimmed and his face smooth. Spoke with a Southern drawl that made him sound more friendly than sinister.

"Yes," she hissed. "I woke up, and there he was just sitting in a chair staring at me. I asked him to leave, and he refused. I wanted to call the police, but he told me to call you first. He's the one who gave me this number. A very strange thing for a murderer to do."

"He's not a murderer, Bubbles. He's there to protect you."

"From what? His beady-eyed glare?"

He did laugh at that. "I've never seen him glare at anyone."

"He's glaring at me."

"Are you wearing your glasses? Maybe you're not seeing him properly."

"Now, how would I be wearing my glasses? I fell in the lake, remember? I got knocked unconscious and nearly drowned. Do you really think I managed to keep track of where my glasses went?" she asked.

"If anyone would be capable of it, you would be."

She laughed, the sound as light and sweet as a spring breeze. "I've missed you, Adam. Why did you wait so long to come back?"

"I guess I needed to figure a few things out."

"And did you manage it?"

"Maybe. How are you feeling?"

"Like I fell in a lake and nearly died," she responded. "I've been thinking about that."

"What?"

"Me falling in the lake."

"What about it?"

"I don't think I fell."

"No?" He kept his tone neutral, but his pulse jumped, his heart galloping in his chest. Honor and River must have noticed the change. They both stepped closer, watching him expectantly.

"I'm pretty careful around the water nowadays. I mean, I swim but only during the day. At my age, you can't be too careful. One fall, one broken hip, and it's all over. You're in a nursing home for the rest of your life, eating pureed peas and lumpy mashed potatoes at every meal and crying because your family never comes to visit."

"Charlotte and I would never make you move into a nursing home. You know that," he reassured her. "And if you decided you wanted to live in one, we'd sneak you in some contraband food."

"What are we talking about here? Steak? Or cupcakes and cookies, candy and pie?"

"All of the above," he responded, and she laughed again.

He waited until she quieted, and then he moved the conversation back to where it had begun. Her concern about her tumble into the lake. "You said you didn't think you fell," he said. "What do you think happened?"

"That's a good question. A very good question. I don't have an answer. I've got nothing in this old brain but a giant-size headache. The doctor said things will start coming back to me, but since he looks like he graduated from elementary school last week, I'm not sure I can believe him."

"I'm sure he knows what he's talking about, and I'm positive he's a little older than middle school age."

"Humph," she replied, her disgust seeping through the phone. "Whether or not that's true isn't the point. The point is, I can't remember a thing after I walked out Charlotte's door. I think, though…" Her voice drifted off, and he didn't try to fill the silence with questions or suggestions. He didn't want to lead her in any direction. He wanted her to remember the truth. Not something that had been planted in her head.

"You know," she murmured. "I feel like I saw someone after that. A man. But I don't remember being afraid, and you'd think I would have been. You'd think if some stranger who wanted to off Charlotte and kill me in the process had been lurking outside, I'd have been terrified. Wouldn't you think that?"

"Yes," he responded, his mind spinning with possibilities.

She could be mistaken and hadn't seen anyone.

She could have seen a stranger and didn't remember her fear.

Or she could have seen someone she knew, someone so familiar she had no reason to be afraid.

"But I don't remember being afraid. Then again, I don't really remember anything. Just walking outside to get Clover and maybe seeing someone." She sighed. "It's all very frustrating. You know how good my memory has always been."

"It will come back to you. Just like the doctor said. For now, try not to worry about it. Just rest and heal. Charlotte and I will be at the hospital later. Is there anything you want us to bring?"

"A grandbaby would be nice, but since the two of you are no longer married, I'll settle for my bed jacket and some toiletries. Charlotte knows what I like, and she has a key to my place."

"I'll have her grab a few things. See you soon, Bubbles," he said, disconnecting the call and sliding the phone into his pocket.

"What's going on?" Honor asked as they

reached the Cadillac. A small rental car was parked behind it, and she unlocked the door and opened it but didn't get in.

"That was Charlotte's neighbor."

"The one who nearly drowned?" she asked, and he nodded.

"She wasn't very happy to have a bodyguard sitting in her room. She said Sam is shifty."

River laughed at that, climbing in behind the wheel of the Cadillac. "If he's shifty, I'd like to know what I am."

"Don't ask Bubbles. She's not known for her subtlety, and you might get your feelings hurt."

He laughed again. "It would take a lot more than an old lady to hurt my feelings."

"What feelings?" Honor asked, and Adam got the impression it was only partly a joke.

"I have plenty, but now isn't the time to discuss them," River replied without any heat. "I'm more interested in hearing what else Bubbles had to say. From this end of the conversation, it sounded like she might have remembered something."

"Maybe. She said she thought she remembered seeing someone when she walked out of Charlotte's house. A man. She wasn't afraid at the time, and she's not sure the memory is real, but she mentioned it, so it's worrying me."

"She nearly drowned, Adam," Honor said. "She has a head injury. The chances of her being right about this are pretty slim."

"Not in my mind. I've known Bubbles for most of my life. She doesn't overstate things, and she doesn't speak unless she's sure about something."

"You *knew* her most of your life," River pointed out. "But you've been away from Whisper Lake for nearly six years. People change a lot in that amount of time."

"Maybe," he agreed as he got in the car.

"You're not convinced," River said as he executed a U-turn and followed Honor's car back toward the cottage.

"I guess I'm not. The way I see it, things add up better if the person Bubbles saw was familiar to her," he replied.

"Want to elaborate on that?" River asked as he pulled into the driveway and parked behind Honor's car.

She got out of her vehicle, waved at them and jogged into the house.

"The killer knows who Charlotte is," Adam said as she disappeared from view. "Despite all the effort we've put into keeping her identity quiet, he's found her."

"Leaks happen."

"True, but it's just as likely that he saw her the night he abducted Bethany. That he recognized her. That he's known all along that she's the one who ruined his plans."

"You think he's coming after her out of revenge?"

"What other motivation would there be? If she'd seen and recognized him, we'd already know his identity, and he'd already be in jail. He's an intelligent person. I'm sure he's thought that through."

"You have a point, but I'm not sure I buy the revenge thing. He's killed nine women. As far as we know, Bethany is his only failure. If I were him, I'd lay low for a while, then go on the hunt again."

"You're putting your ability to reason on him, River. The guy isn't killing because he's filled with logic and sensibility. He's killing because he's sick. His brain doesn't work the same way as yours or mine. In his mind, he didn't fail because he made mistakes. He failed because of Charlotte. The rage he's experienced because of that isn't going to be extinguished until he makes her pay." He stated the facts without adding any emotion to them, without explaining just how terrifying he found them.

"There could be something more to it," River said as he opened the door and got out of the car.

"What's that?"

"Bethany fits the profile of the Night Stalker's victims perfectly."

"Right."

"Maybe she's been the target all along." River tossed the thought out, and it took a second for Adam to realize what he'd said, what he was implying.

They'd already reached the front door, but Adam didn't open it. "You're saying that every other victim was a replacement for her?" he asked, and River shrugged.

"You're the profiler, Adam. You tell me if it makes sense. The way I see things, Bethany's case is the one-off, the thing that doesn't make sense. Why go to big-city hospitals every other time, and then suddenly decide to hunt close to home? Why change things up now when his other methods have proved successful?"

"Bethany got engaged a few months ago," Adam said, thinking through the information he had, plugging it into the situation River was outlining.

"Don't most couples post the announcement in the paper? Maybe our guy saw the announcement and panicked."

"Some do, but even if Bethany and her fiancé didn't put an announcement in the paper, people in town would have known they were planning to get married. News travels fast in Whisper Lake."

"So, let's say the Night Stalker has been obsessed with Bethany. Let's say each one of the women he killed was someone he'd hoped could take her place and give him the relationship he's been craving. None of them worked out. They all disappointed him, and so he had to kill them." River's voice nearly vibrated with the force of his excitement. He was onto something, and he knew it.

Adam knew it, too. He could feel the truth, sense the way it all fit together.

"That would explain the length of time he held some of them prisoner. The ones who fulfilled his fantasy the best lived the longest," he said.

"If that was the case, what would he do if he found out Bethany was getting married?" River asked.

"He'd probably decide it was time to give the real thing a go. He'd do what he'd been wanting to all along. He'd kidnap Bethany in the hopes of convincing her that he was a better choice than her fiancé."

"And if someone got in the way of that? If someone stopped him from achieving the goal? Then revenge would probably be a whole lot more important than laying low."

"If you're right, then Bethany knows the Night Stalker," Adam said, his body humming with adrenaline, his mind sharply focused. "Let's see if Wren can get a list from her. Men she knows who seem to hang in the background a lot. Maybe are always around when she isn't expecting them. The Night Stalker isn't going to be the kind of guy who's overtly trying to get her attention. He's more the type to play the friendship card, call just to say hi. He may even have a girlfriend or a wife."

"Wonder how many names she can come up with," River said as he opened the door.

"If it's the right name, all we need is one," Adam responded, hurrying inside.

SEVEN

Once upon a time, early morning had been Charlotte's favorite time of day. She'd loved sitting on the back deck watching the sun rise over distant mountains. In the winter, she'd nurse a cup of coffee while snow drifted across the frozen earth. In the spring, she'd listen to the birds greet the day. Each season had been her favorite, every sunrise something to celebrate. Even when she'd been a young teen with an attitude, she'd appreciated the expectant hush of the waking day.

After Daniel's birth, she'd taken him outside with her. She'd bundle him in an old quilt if it were cold. When it was hot, he'd be in a diaper and onesie, his chubby cheeks bathed in gold from the rising sun. On the days when Adam wasn't working, they'd be out there together, sometimes talking, sometimes not. Always sitting shoulder to shoulder in the old swing that her grandfather had hung decades ago.

As the years passed and Daniel's differences became obvious, mornings had become even more precious. That was the time of day when he'd seemed less stressed and more relaxed. He'd sit in her lap while it swayed, humming quietly. No head banging. No screaming. No tearing at his hair. He was peaceful in the early morning, and she'd been peaceful with him.

Now she hated the hours before dawn.

She hated the emptiness, the silence, the sickening knowledge that she was about to face another sunrise without the two people she loved most. She tried to sleep through those hours, but her body only knew the rhythm it had always lived by. No matter how late she stayed up, no matter how far she ran or how hard she worked out, her eyes still opened before dawn.

Today was no exception.

She'd been lying in bed for an hour before she fell asleep, waiting for Adam, River and Honor to return from the logging camp. She'd convinced Savannah to sleep in the guest room, and then she'd retreated to her bedroom. She hadn't bothered to change. She'd just lain on top of the covers, telling herself she wasn't going to fall asleep.

Of course, she had.

Now she was awake, bathed in sweat, the remnants of a nightmare clawing at the edges of her mind. She couldn't remember the details. She could only remember the fear.

She glanced at the clock on the bedside table, frowning when she saw the time—2:00 a.m. wasn't her favorite time to be awake. Especially if she wasn't going to be able to get back to sleep.

And she wasn't.

That was the way it worked. She slept for a short period of time, and then she was awake. No matter how much she didn't want to be.

Resigned to her fate, she sat up, surprised when a blanket pooled around her hips. She hadn't had it when she'd fallen asleep. Had Wren walked into the room and put the blanket over her? Or maybe, Charlotte had walked to the linen closet herself, grabbed a blanket and returned to the room. She didn't normally sleepwalk. But then, she didn't normally nearly get killed twice in a two-week time span.

She flicked on the lamp and glanced at Clover. He was lying in his bed a few feet away, his tail thumping rhythmically as he watched her. He was used to being woken at all hours of the night, and he stood as she climbed out of bed.

She folded the blanket carefully, laying it across the footboard. She could hear voices drifting in from under the door. Not just Wren talking on the phone. There were multiple voices. Male and female.

Adam?

She thought she could hear him, and she walked to the door, pulling it open and stepping into the hall. Clover padded along beside her as she made her way down the short corridor. He didn't seem worried about the people who were talking, but then, Clover wasn't a nervous dog. If people were inside the house, he'd assume they belonged there.

She could see the living room as she approached the end of the narrow corridor. It seemed filled with people. FBI agents. Local police. State police. All of them were crowded into a space that wasn't meant for more than five.

"What's going on?" she asked, and they all turned in her direction.

"Just going over some plans." Adam spoke for the group, his voice drawing her attention.

She met his eyes, forgot for a moment that they weren't the only people in the room. He looked like a more mature version of the boy she'd first seen in seventh-grade biology. His dark hair was shorter, his skin a shade darker, his shoulders and arms filled out with muscle, but his eyes still flashed with curiosity and interest when he looked at her.

"You're back," she said, and he smiled the kind of slow easy smile that had always made her toes curl and her pulse jump.

That hadn't changed.

Nothing, she thought, *really had*.

Except for the fact that they weren't together anymore. Their marriage had dissolved, and Adam had walked away with nothing but a suitcase filled with his clothes, half the money in their checking account and the wedding ring she'd bought him a few days before they'd married. The thick gold band had symbolized forever.

Had he sold it? Stuck it in a drawer somewhere and forgotten about it?

She knew it didn't matter. What he'd done with it, where he'd put it, had nothing to do with her or this moment, but she couldn't help wondering.

"And you're still half-asleep," he responded. "I can tell by the glassy look in your eyes. Want some coffee?"

"I'd rather be filled in on the plans you're

making," she said, shifting her attention to a man in a state police uniform, then to the wall, to the window near the front door. The floor. The ceiling. Anywhere but Adam.

"Wren? Are you okay with that?" he said, and Charlotte's gaze jumped to him again, her heart giving a quick hard beat of acknowledgment as she looked at his dark gray eyes.

"Sure. She's part of it, so she needs to know," Wren responded. She was in the kitchen again, sitting at the table with Honor, both of them staring at computer monitors.

"Part of what?" Charlotte stepped farther into the room, eyeing the men and women who were there. Several were wearing Whisper Lake Sheriff's Department uniforms. She recognized their faces, but she couldn't put names to any of them. Most of the men and women who'd been working for the town police department when Daniel died were gone now. They'd either moved to bigger cities or switched careers. They were the only police officers she'd ever gotten to know well. They'd been the ones to reassure her when Daniel first wandered away from his sitter, telling her that he'd probably gone to the neighbors or started walking to town, trying to find her and Adam.

Later, when divers had pulled his body

from the lake, they'd been the ones to break the news, to hold her up when she'd nearly collapsed, to bring her juice and call her grandmother and bring Adam to identify the body.

She shuddered, and she knew Adam noticed; he was watching her intently, his gaze never wavering.

"You okay?" he asked.

"A goose walked over my grave," she responded, borrowing one of her grandmother's old sayings.

"You sound like Mildred," he replied, a soft smile easing the hard lines and angles of his face. "I'm sorry I missed the funeral. I was in another state, working a case. I didn't get your note until a month later. By that time, it was too late. I did send you—"

"You don't have to explain," she cut him off. She'd gotten the sympathy card. She'd tucked it in a box with all the others and tried to tell herself that she hadn't expected more from him. "It was a long time ago."

"Three years isn't that long," he said.

"You were going to tell me about your plans?" She changed the subject, and Adam let her.

"We think that the Night Stalker is someone Bethany and Bubbles both know. Someone who lives close. Who would be very familiar to them."

"If that's the case, I probably know him, too."

"That's what we're hoping. We asked Bethany to make a list of men she has contact with who fit the guy's criminal profile. She's already provided that for us. The next step is getting a list from you and from Bubbles."

"A list from me would be long. I know lots of men who live in Whisper Lake and the surrounding areas. I work at the community college and I run dog-training classes. That puts me in touch with a lot of people."

"You also visit hospitals and elderly care facilities," Wren reminded her. As if she'd forgotten her own story.

"That's true," she conceded. "But the people I interact with there aren't in any shape to do what the Night Stalker does."

"We're not just talking about the patients and clients," Adam said. "We're talking about family members of the people you interact with. Employees of the facilities. Doctors, nurses, therapists."

"Like I said, that would be a very long list."

"It still needs to be made." Honor joined the conversation, her attention still focused on the computer screen. "Besides, you won't be listing everyone. You'll be listing men who fit a certain profile."

"Maybe someone can explain that profile to me?" Charlotte suggested, not quite able to hide the sarcasm in her voice. She didn't mind making the list. As a matter of fact, she welcomed the opportunity to help find the suspect, but she hadn't been kidding when she'd said her list would be long. She interacted with hundreds of people during her workweek, dozens more when she and Clover visited the hospital and elderly care facilities.

"I'll go over it with you in the car," Adam said, walking to the coat closet and opening it.

"The car?" she repeated.

"You wanted to visit Bubbles?" He eyed the interior of the closet for a couple of seconds and then pulled out the winter coat she'd inherited from her grandmother. Mildred had loved fashion, and she'd kept a lot of the clothes she'd acquired during her lifetime. Most of it was in trunks in the storage room upstairs, but the 1940s wool coat had had a timeless quality that Charlotte loved. She wore the coat all the time in the winter, but that wasn't something Adam could have known. Mildred had passed away two years after he'd left.

The doctors had said she'd died from a heart attack.

That might be true, but Charlotte believed that Mildred's heart had broken long before it had failed. First, she'd lost Robert. Then Daniel. Then Adam and Charlotte had split. Mildred had been living in a cute retirement village in Arizona for several years by then, pursuing a dream she and Robert had once made together. She'd come back for Daniel's funeral. She'd returned for a few days when Adam left. Both times, she'd told Charlotte how much she enjoyed life in Phoenix, but she'd looked older, sadder, frailer.

Charlotte had noticed.

She'd tried to get Mildred to move back to the cottage, but her grandmother had refused to return. She'd died in a hospital in Phoenix an hour before Charlotte could get to her.

"Charlotte?" Adam prodded. "Have you changed your mind about visiting Bubbles?"

"It's a little early in the morning," she said, her mouth dry with memories and sorrow.

"I don't think Bubbles will mind," he responded, holding out the coat so that she could slide into it. His fingers were warm against her nape as he straightened the collar, and she felt something dormant spring to life again. It zipped through her, lodging itself in that space in her heart. The one that had only and always been reserved for Adam.

She shivered, stepping back.

"Bubbles might not mind," she commented. "But I'm not sure the hospital will want us there. Visiting hours ended a long time ago."

"Don't worry about that," Wren said. "Everything is cleared. Besides, Bubbles has been awake and asking for you for a while."

"She has been?"

"Have you checked your phone? I'm sure you've gotten more messages than any of us, but she's managed to call me and Adam several times."

Surprised, Charlotte patted her pockets, trying to find her cell phone. When she didn't, she glanced around the room, looking for her purse.

"Right here." Adam reached into the closet again and pulled out her handbag. "You left it on the couch. I didn't want it getting lost in the shuffle of people moving through the house."

"Thanks," she mumbled, digging through it until she found her cell phone. Sure enough, there were several voice mail messages. She listened as she grabbed keys from the hook near the front door and dropped them into her purse.

The first and second messages were from Bubbles, her voice shaky and hoarse. She mentioned a beady-eyed man who wouldn't leave her alone and asked Charlotte to pick up toiletries from her house.

"Was that her?" Adam asked.

"Yes. She wants me to get a few things from her place."

"We'll stop there on the way out."

She nodded, still listening as the third voice mail message began.

"Hi, Charlotte," a woman said. "This is Anna Randel from Pine Valley Center. We have you and Clover on the schedule for next week, but I was wondering if you could come sometime this week, as well. The residents love your visits, and one of them has been asking for you. Give me a call. Maybe we can work something out?"

"Was that Bubbles, too? She sure hasn't lost her persistence and determination, has she?" Adam said, grabbing his coat from the back of a chair. She'd forgotten that he did that. Forgotten how much it had amused her that a man as neat and organized as he was constantly left his coat dangling from whatever available surface he could find.

"She hasn't, but that wasn't her. It was someone from an Alzheimer's center Clover and I visit. She wanted to know if we could come this week."

"Probably not," Adam responded, steering her toward the door. "Until we find the Night Stalker, I prefer you stay out of the public eye."

"And yet," Wren muttered, shrugging into her coat, "we're bringing her to the hospital to visit Bubbles."

"We've had the hospital under surveillance for hours," Adam responded. "Sam. Local and state police. Plenty of law enforcement presence, and the Night Stalker isn't going to risk being caught. He'll stay away and wait for an opportunity to strike without risk."

"Let's make sure not to give him one. River, how about you head over to Bubbles's house? Check things out? We'll ride over in the car. Bubbles has a portico that will offer us some cover, but let's make this quick. I want to spend as little time outside as possible." Wren glanced at her watch. "We'll have ten minutes to gather the items Bubbles wants. Then we're out of there."

"I need to let Clover out before we go," Charlotte cut in, glancing at the dog. He'd made himself comfortable on the couch, squeezed between two state police officers. They were petting him, of course. No one could resist Clover's soft coat and sweet face.

"How about we let someone else do that?" Adam suggested. "I don't know about you, but I'm anxious to hear what Bubbles has to say about what happened."

"I'll let him out," one of the Whisper Lake police officers said. He looked very young and very familiar, his bright blue eyes surrounded by thick black lashes that any woman would be proud of.

Charlotte studied him for a moment, trying to place the face. "Were you one of my students?" she guessed.

He nodded. "I'm Josh Henry. I was in your Calc 100 class last year. I attended a couple of your review sessions, too. Thanks to those, I passed the class and got my Associate of Arts degree."

"I think that probably had more to do with you than with my review classes," she said. She remembered him now—always in the front row. Eager and quick. Math hadn't been his strength, but he'd studied hard and pursued extra help when he needed it. Now he'd graduated, joined the police force and was making her feel way older than she probably should.

Life was passing, and she was letting it happen.

When had she stopped being an active participant?

When had her carefully crafted routine become her definition of living?

She frowned, watching as Josh grabbed the leash that was hanging near the back door, hooked it to Clover's collar and stepped outside with him.

"Was I ever that young and energetic?" she whispered, and Adam smiled.

"You still are that young, Charlotte."

"He's a teenager," she protested.

"He's twenty-five. Three years younger than you."

"And you know this how?"

"We check backgrounds on everyone who's working with us," he responded.

"Are we ready?" River cut in.

"Whenever you are," Adam replied.

"Now works. I'll meet you guys over there." He stepped outside and shut the door.

"What about the key?" Charlotte asked, pulling her key chain from her purse.

"He won't need it," Adam assured her, cupping her elbow and walking her to the door. She couldn't feel the warmth of his skin through her coat sleeve, but she could feel the gentle strength of his grip, the subtle way he was offering support.

She wanted to cling to him the way she used to.

She wanted to step in close and feel his biceps brushing against her shoulder as they moved. She wanted so many things she could never have—a do-over, a second chance, three seconds to go back to the day she'd let him walk away and beg him to stay. She'd been too proud back then, too broken, too angry.

Now…

Now she was only sad for what they'd lost when they'd given up on each other.

"Are you sure? Bubbles doesn't keep a spare key anywhere," she said, her voice husky with longing and regret.

He heard it. She knew he did.

His brow furrowed, and he studied her face, his fingers still on her arm. He looked like he might say something, but his gaze shifted to Wren and then to the group of law enforcement officers who crowded into her living room.

"I'm sure," he finally said. "River has a way with locks. They tend to open for him without much trouble."

"That sounds illegal," she murmured.

"Only if he gets caught," Wren said. "Let's go."

She opened the door, letting cold moist air sweep in. The rain hadn't let up. It was still falling steadily as Adam nudged Charlotte out onto the front porch.

"You said someone from an Alzheimer's

facility called and asked you to come for a visit, right?" Wren asked as she opened the Cadillac's back door and gestured for Charlotte to slide in.

"Yes. Why?"

"Just thinking that it's an interesting proposition." Wren slid into the driver's seat, starting the engine as Adam settled into the seat beside Charlotte.

"What's interesting about it?" he asked.

"If it's a place we can secure easily, it might not be a bad idea," Wren responded, putting the car in gear.

"You're kidding, right?" Adam responded.

"Why would I be?"

"Because the Night Stalker wants her dead. The only safe place for her is somewhere far away from any place he's familiar with."

"The best way to catch a rat is to bait the trap with something he likes," Wren responded.

Adam stilled.

Charlotte could feel the tension in his muscles, the stiff way he held himself. "No," he growled.

"It's not your decision to make," Wren responded calmly. "We're going to discuss the options and weigh the risks. We'll make the decision as a team."

"Without consulting me?" Charlotte broke in, her pulse racing. If she was going to be used as Night Stalker bait, she'd at least like to have some input into how the plan would go down.

"Of course we'll consult you. If you're not comfortable with the plan, we'll change it."

"There is no plan," Adam grumbled. "And if the one you're thinking of really involves prancing Charlotte all over town like she's a hot fudge sundae at an ice cream lover's convention, there is never going to be one."

"A hot fudge sundae at an ice cream lover's convention?" Charlotte repeated, laughter bubbling out and filling the car.

"You did always say that I had a way with words," he responded, and she realized he was watching her, his tension gone, his expression unreadable.

She looked into his eyes, because he was there and she was, and the years apart didn't seem to matter nearly as much as the time they'd spent together, the secrets they'd shared, the life they'd planned.

Her laughter died, and she touched his jaw, her fingers running over prickly stubble and warm skin.

She shouldn't have done it.

She knew that, but she hadn't been able to stop herself.

Her hand dropped away, and he captured it, running his thumb across her knuckles.

"I missed your laughter, Charlotte," he said so quietly she almost didn't hear.

"I missed *you*," she responded, the words coming from a place so deep in her soul that she hadn't even realized they were there or that she was going to say them.

"What I mean—" she began.

"Don't ruin it, okay?" He cut her off, squeezing her hand gently before releasing it. "Just let it be what it is."

"What's that?" she asked as Wren turned into Bubbles's driveway.

"A truth we both should have spoken a long time ago," he replied.

She wanted to ask him what he meant, but the car stopped, and he got out, the moment lost. Just like so many others had been.

When he reached for her hand, she took it, though, and when he held on to it as they walked to Bubbles's house, she didn't make any attempt to pull away.

This was where she should have been all along.

This was what she'd been missing for five and a half years.

This was what she should have fought for, what she hadn't dared believe she could keep.

Maybe she should have trusted a little more, believed a little harder. Maybe she should have had more faith that God could fill the silences between them with peace and comfort and love, but her faith had been weak at best. Nonexistent at worst. It had taken losing Daniel to understand how much she needed to believe that God was there. She'd been lost in her sorrow, consumed by her despair. Reaching out to Adam had been as impossible as going back in time and saving her son.

Now that she was through the worst of it and the pain was more a nagging ache than stabbing agony, she could see how easy it would have been to agree to Adam's plan. Right now, in this moment, if he asked again, if he told her once more that he had to leave to heal, she'd go with him so they could heal together.

But, of course, it was too late.

The time for making that decision had passed, and now she could only move forward in the direction she'd been heading before Adam stepped back into her life.

She tugged her hand from his as he opened Bubbles's door, stepping into the cool musty house alone, and telling herself that was exactly how she was meant to be.

To Adam, Bubbles's house had always felt like a mansion. Even now, after years of being away and seeing plenty of bigger, grander houses, it felt that way.

He followed Charlotte through the foyer and up the curved stairs that led to the second floor. Wren was right behind him, her footsteps light on the carpeted tread. He wasn't sure where River was. Probably somewhere in the bowels of the house, checking to make sure no one was lurking there.

"This place is creepy," Wren huffed as they reached the landing.

"What makes you say that?" he asked, and she pointed to an old armchair that sat against the wall. Several porcelain dolls were piled on top of it, their glass eyes staring lifelessly.

"That," she responded.

"They're dolls."

"Dolls belong in little kids' playrooms. Not on chairs at the top of stair landings."

"If you don't like the dolls, don't come in Bubbles's room. She collects them," Charlotte said as she pushed open a door at the end of the hall.

He walked in behind her, stopping short

when he realized just how many dolls the elderly woman had acquired.

He whistled under his breath, scanning the shelves and chairs and bed, all of them piled high with her collection. "Wow," he said, because it was all he could manage.

"I know, right?" she responded, opening Bubbles's wardrobe and grabbing a small carryall from it.

"When did this happen?" he asked, because it hadn't been this way when he'd left. In all the time he'd known her, Bubbles's house had never been anything other than pristine. He'd learned to be neat from her. He'd learned the value of clean and organized spaces by helping her dust and polish and put things away.

Cleanliness is next to Godliness, and it also keeps a person from being embarrassed when people stop by unexpectedly.

That had been her motto, and he'd embraced it, because neat was better than the clutter he'd lived with at home. The house he'd shared with his mother had been just like this—filled with stuff. Only the stuff had been mostly trash, dirty dishes and cigarette butts.

"I don't really know." Charlotte pulled a gauzy nightgown from the wardrobe and folded it neatly. "It wasn't like this when

Daniel died, and then it was. That's all I can tell you."

"She was filling up the emptiness," he said, lifting one of the old porcelain dolls and touching a crack on its face.

"She could have filled it with puppies," Wren said, peering in the open doorway. "Or kittens. Or even goldfish. Why dolls?"

"I think Bubbles always wanted children. She was so happy when Daniel was born. He was the grandson she never thought she'd have." Charlotte opened a dresser drawer and pulled out clothes that she tucked carefully into the bag. "She used to buy him trucks and cars from flea markets. Remember, Adam? She loved bringing him surprises."

Yeah. He remembered.

He also remembered the way Bubbles had looked when she'd seen the baby for the first time—his face still red and pinched, his eyes clenched shut. She'd bustled into the room with balloons and a giant stuffed dog, all business and ready to get on with things. And then she'd seen Daniel; she'd touched his fisted hand and downy hair. When Charlotte had handed him to her, she'd held him like he was the most precious gift she'd ever received.

She'd loved him.

Somehow Adam had let himself forget that.

"I remember," he said, setting the doll down.

"You guys almost done?" River called, and something in his voice cleared Adam's head, made him push the memories aside and remember exactly why they were in Bubbles's room.

"Are we?" he asked, and Charlotte nodded.

"Just let me grab a few things from the bathroom." She jogged past him, the carryall bouncing against her slim hip. She'd changed into yoga pants, a fitted T-shirt and a long cardigan. He'd noticed that when he'd walked into her room and found her sleeping. She'd been curled up on her side, her body tense even in slumber, the clothes emphasizing her reed-thin frame, the narrowness of her hips and shoulders.

She'd looked fragile and vulnerable, and he'd grabbed a blanket from the linen closet to cover her, because there'd been nothing else he could do. He'd given up his right to watch her sleep. He'd abdicated his role as protector, confidant and friend.

"Let's go," River said, suddenly on the landing, his firearm out, his muscles tense.

"What's wrong?" Adam asked, and he shook his head.

"I don't know. Just a feeling that something isn't right. All the windows and doors were locked up tight, but the cellar door wasn't bolted from the inside."

"I doubt Bubbles spends much time down there," Adam said, but he was already moving toward the bathroom, ready to grab Charlotte and leave.

"Maybe not, but Charlotte told us that Bubbles is a little paranoid. That she's obsessive about locking doors."

He was right. Charlotte had mentioned that more than once when they'd discussed the open door at the cottage.

"Your feelings are usually impeccable, River. If you're worried, so am I," Wren said. "Let's get Charlotte and head out." Wren strode toward the stairs, obviously planning to assess the situation herself.

She didn't have a chance.

Something exploded, the force of it shaking the house on its foundation. Smoke billowed through the cracks in the wood floorboards, snaking up and tainting the air.

Everyone was moving. Charlotte running from the bathroom, a brush in her hand, the old wool coat billowing out around her. Wren sprinting downstairs, gun in hand. Adam and River flanking Charlotte and rushing her toward the servant staircase in the back of the house.

They didn't have a plan.

They didn't need one.

They each knew the priority. Get the civilian out unharmed.

Adam had been in plenty of dangerous situations. He'd freed hostages and led them to safety. He'd been in gun battles where innocent people were being used as shields. Every life he'd saved had been important. Every innocent person he'd helped had been worth the effort.

But this was Charlotte.

The woman who'd once held his heart.

He couldn't fail her. Not again.

He flung open the door that led into the narrow stairwell.

No smoke there. Just chilly air and darkness.

"Move!" he shouted, nearly lifting Charlotte off her feet as he propelled her through the opening.

EIGHT

The house shook again as they stumbled down the dark staircase, and Charlotte's foot slipped, her legs going out from under her. If Adam's arm hadn't been around her waist, she'd have fallen, but he yanked her back up, tugging her closer to his side.

"We're almost there," he said, his voice steady and calm.

"How do you know?" *Her* voice was shaky and panicked. She didn't know what was going on, but it was bad. Really bad. She could smell smoke, taste it in the air. Worse, the house seemed to have shifted, the old staircase uneven, the floorboards seeming to give as she stepped on them.

"I used to work for Bubbles, remember? I've used this stairway hundreds of times. There are twenty-three steps, and we just hit the last one." He reached out, and she could see his arm in the darkness, his hand feeling for the door that led into the kitchen.

He found it. Finally. Pushed it open.

The kitchen was dark. No lights from the appliances. No soft tick of the clock that usually hung from the wall. The house felt silent, empty and cold, but the floor vibrated beneath Charlotte's feet, the old wood unstable.

"Careful. If the foundation is shot, some of the support beams might be gone, too." River stepped in front of her, leading the way into the room, moving slowly and cautiously. Below them, old timber creaked and groaned, the soft hiss of the old radiator mixing with the whistling sound of steam being pushed too rapidly through a narrow opening.

"That doesn't sound good," she whispered, afraid if she spoke too loudly the entire house would tumble in on them.

"None of this is good," Adam replied.

"What happened? What's going on?"

"My guess is that the Night Stalker planted explosives. Maybe he planned to use a detonator to set them off when Bubbles returned."

"He didn't do a very good job if they exploded before she got here."

"I don't think he was finished," River said, testing the floorboard in front of him before putting his weight on it.

"What do you mean?"

"I think he was here when I arrived. The house felt off, but the front and back doors were locked. All the windows were locked. I was able to pick a lock on a side door, and I was fairly quiet when I arrived, but if the Night Stalker was down in the basement, he'd have heard my footsteps as I was walking through the house."

"So, you interrupted him, and he left?" She stumbled over something—maybe a chair—and Adam pulled her closer. She could feel his heart thrumming in his chest, feel the tension in his muscles. Hear the soft controlled breaths he was taking.

"He didn't go far. He was probably in the woods when you arrived, realized that this was a golden opportunity to get rid of you and set off the detonator." River was moving a little more quickly now, making his way through the room, his body silhouetted by moonlight that streamed in through the kitchen window.

Charlotte and Adam followed, picking their way across the kitchen, following the path River was forging. Smoke streamed up from cracks in the wood floor, drifting into the darkness in lazy tendrils of inky blackness that stung Charlotte's nose and throat.

"You doing okay?" Adam asked.

"Dandy," she replied, and she was certain that he smiled at her through the darkness.

River had reached the three-season room that jutted off the back of the house. Decades ago, it had been a porch, but one of Bubbles's grandparents had closed it in and created a room that could be used most of the year. There were windows on three sides. Any one of them would give the Night Stalker a clear view of the interior. Charlotte hesitated at the threshold, scanning the windows and searching the landscape beyond them. She didn't want to escape an explosion and get killed by a sniper's bullet.

She also didn't want to stand in the darkness too terrified to act.

"It's okay," Adam murmured in her ear, nudging her into the room. The floor was more stable there, the air clearer. Unlike the rest of the house, it was built on bedrock rather than a basement.

"Okay? He could still be out there," she responded. "We need to go see if we can stop him before he takes off." She would have darted for the door, but he pulled her up short.

"Wren is already searching for him. I'm pretty certain a dozen other law enforcement officers are on their way."

"You called this in?"

"I didn't have to. The explosion was loud enough to be heard at your place. Come on. We're clearing out."

"And going where?"

"To the hospital. Like we originally planned."

"But—"

"Let's go," River snapped, opening the exterior door and stepping outside. Adam nudged Charlotte forward, and she followed, sandwiched between the men as if they could block a bullet that might fly toward her, keep her safe from the maniac who wanted her dead.

Her and Bubbles dead.

The thought left her cold with fear and rage.

"What if he's on his way to the hospital?" She spoke out loud. "If he's trying to kill Bubbles, isn't that the first place he should have gone?"

"Why do you think he hasn't already been there? It's been five hours since she was admitted. Plenty of time for him to get there and back," Adam responded as they rounded the side of the house and hurried to the Cadillac.

Sirens were screaming, emergency lights flashing on the road. Help was on the way, but it was too late for the house. The structure was listing to the right, sinking into the ground it had been built on.

Bubbles would be heartbroken, and the

thought of that only added fuel to the fire of her rage.

"He destroyed everything she owns," she said, her gaze on the house and the flames that were shooting from the right corner of the foundation.

"But he didn't destroy her." Adam opened the back door of the Cadillac, nearly shoving her in.

Wren had left the keys in the ignition, and River jumped into the driver's seat, revving the engine impatiently as Adam climbed into the back seat.

"Ready?" River asked, already gunning the engine, the Cadillac jumping forward and speeding toward the road.

Charlotte scanned the trees and brush as they sped past, looking for signs that the Night Stalker might still be there. As if he'd be foolish enough to wait around.

Then again, his truck had been impounded.

It might have been difficult to find another ride.

"He'd have to have a vehicle to get to the hospital." She spoke into tense silence, and River grunted in reply.

"What's that mean?" she asked.

"It means, he probably does have a vehicle. That truck was what he used to transport his victims. It's not the car he uses every day," Adam explained.

"Are you sure?"

"As sure as I can be. The Night Stalker travels a lot. It's hard to do that if you don't have money."

"Is that part of the profile you plan to give me?" she asked, and he nodded.

"What else?" she asked, already thinking through her list of friends and contacts. She knew plenty of people who had money. Whisper Lake was a small town, but it wasn't a poor one.

"More than likely, he's in his mid to late thirties. Caucasian. An introvert, but not unfriendly. The kind of guy who wouldn't stand out as the leader of a group, would never be the life of the party, but wouldn't strike anyone as overly odd, either."

"So, not like Mackey Sheridan?" Mackey currently owned a high-end butcher shop on Main Street. If rumors were to be believed, he'd made a killing capitalizing on people's desire for grass-fed beef and free-range chicken.

"Mackey?" Adam asked.

"Macmillan Sheridan? He graduated the same year as us but was a couple of years younger, because his mother insisted he be allowed to skip first and third grade."

"The redheaded kid with the thick glasses and the three-piece suits?"

"That's him. Only, he's an adult now. He wears contacts, and he owns a butcher shop on Main Street."

"I thought he left town."

"He did. He hopped on a plane a couple of hours after we graduated and didn't return until his mother died a few years ago."

"How many years?" River asked.

"Four? Five? I'm not sure. I lost track of time for a while."

"We need to check into that," River said. "Adam, do you want to contact Honor? Ask her to do a little research on the guy? See if he owns property on or around the lake?"

"I'm texting her now." He'd pulled out his phone and was typing rapidly.

"I don't think Mackey is the Night Stalker," she said quickly. "He's nothing like what you described. That's why I mentioned him, because I wanted to make sure he wasn't the kind of person you wanted on my list."

"As far as we've been able to ascertain," Adam said, still typing the text message, "the Night Stalker kidnapped and murdered his first victim five years ago."

She went cold at the words, her mind rushing backward, trying to put a timeline on

Jenny Sheridan's death, on her funeral, on the day that Mackey had returned.

Not for his mother's funeral.

People had talked about that for months afterward.

He'd come to clean out her house and to live in it.

"You've gone quiet," River commented. "What are you thinking?"

"He didn't attend his mother's funeral. A few weeks later, he showed up and started cleaning out her house. He hired contractors, had an addition put on the back that was bigger than the original house. People wondered where he got the money, but he wasn't very friendly, and he wasn't willing to answer questions, so eventually he was left alone."

"Not friendly, huh?" Adam typed something into his phone and then shoved it in his pocket.

"No. That's why I don't think he's the Night Stalker. You said the guy would be friendly and wouldn't stand out in a bad way."

"Profiles aren't set in stone. They're educated conjecture. It's possible I was off base."

"You've never been before," River said. "Not when it comes to your work."

"There's always a first time. I asked Honor to check into Mackey's background and his property, see if he's on the list Bethany provided. If he is, that's another point against him."

"I think he's too obvious," Charlotte said, blushing when Adam smiled. "Not that I know anything about any of this."

"You know a lot about the people who live here," he responded, tucking a strand of hair behind her ear. She'd cut it short a few months after he'd left, because he'd loved playing with her hair, running his fingers through it, telling her how beautiful it was. "Is there anyone you can think of who works in the medical field and travels a lot?" he asked.

"Every doctor who works at the trauma center travels. They guest lecture at county hospitals and give classes on level-one trauma. It's part of their contract." She'd heard that from a friend who was a surgeon at Whisper Lake Medical Center.

"That's a whole lot of people we just added to our list," River said as he turned onto the road that led to the medical center.

"I don't think he's a doctor," Adam responded.

"Because his time would be too limited?" River asked.

"Because he'd probably have more creative ways to use a knife or scalpel if he were a doctor, or even a nurse," Adam answered, and Charlotte's skin crawled, her mind jumping back to the night she'd heard Bethany scream.

If she hadn't been awake, if she hadn't adopted Clover, if Clover hadn't whined…

Bethany would be dead.

Or she'd be trapped in a madman's prison, tortured, terrified and alone.

"It's okay," Adam said. "You're okay. Whatever you're thinking about can't hurt you anymore."

He touched her wrist, and she realized her hands were fisted so tightly her nails were digging into her palm, the warmth of his fingers both strange and familiar.

"I was thinking about the Night Stalker," she murmured, her cheeks warm from his touch and from her reaction to it. "He's pretty determined to hurt me."

"And I'm even more determined to keep you safe." He dropped his arm around her shoulders, tugging her into his side the way he'd done hundreds of times before.

In another lifetime.

When they were young and naive and thought life would always be what it was.

But this was now. This was after. This was when there was too much stuff between them for them ever to be close. She understood that, but she couldn't make herself move away.

Instead, she let her head drop to his shoulder, let him smooth her hair the way he'd always done, let herself stay right where she was as River pulled into the hospital parking garage and parked the car.

He was getting too close to Charlotte. Adam knew it, and he couldn't make himself care. He'd fallen in love with her years ago, and he'd never fallen out of it. He'd left her because he was a coward, but he'd grown up a lot in the years since. Returning to Whisper Lake hadn't been something he'd expected to do, seeing Charlotte again hadn't been something he'd thought he'd wanted or needed.

Sure, he'd thought about apologizing. He'd wondered how she was doing, found himself thinking about her a little more than he should have been, but he'd put their relationship behind him. He'd been content with that.

And now he was back in Whisper Lake, and he was beginning to realize how much he'd given up when he'd left. Not just Charlotte, but his community, his church, his friends.

Losing Daniel had been the hardest thing he'd ever gone through, but he could have grieved in a place where people loved and supported him. Instead, he'd run from the memories and from the people he cared about most. He'd cut them off as if they were responsible for his pain.

River got out of the Cadillac, shooting Adam a hard look as he opened Charlotte's door. He didn't approve of the closeness between them, and he was letting Adam know it.

"You'd better watch yourself," he commented as Adam climbed out of the car. "These kinds of things can get messy."

"What things?" Charlotte asked.

"Just making a comment," River responded. "We ready to head inside? The less time we spend out in the open, the happier I'll be."

He took Charlotte's arm, leading her toward the medical center.

It was a protective gesture. One that Adam respected. Even though he was certain the person River was protecting Charlotte from was him.

"I've been thinking about the profile you created," she said as they walked into the building.

"What about it?"

"You said that the guy you're looking for is a professional, right? In the medical field? That he travels a lot? That he has money?"

"Right."

"I actually do know someone like that," she said.

Just like that.

No inflection in her voice.

No excitement. Just a statement of fact. That, more than anything, made Adam's blood pulse with adrenaline. He'd heard the same tone from victims who'd been resolute and certain, who knew their attacker but doubted anyone would believe them if they told the truth.

Whoever Charlotte was thinking of, he was someone well respected by the community.

"Who?"

"Liam Jeffers. He's an assistant youth pastor at the church. A really nice guy, but I don't know him very well. He mostly keeps to himself." They reached a bank of elevators and River punched the call button.

He didn't speak.

Adam didn't, either.

This was the time when they were most likely to make a mistake, to shut down the victim without meaning to. Their enthusiasm and excitement for new information could be overwhelming to someone who was still feeling her way through, trying to make sense of what had happened to her. One wrong word, one careless phrase, and the nugget of truth that Charlotte planned to give them would be hidden away again.

The doors slid open, and they stepped onto the elevator. All of them silent. Charlotte must have known they were waiting her out.

She sighed, leaning her hip against the wall. "I wouldn't have thought of him except that I was at Pine Valley last week, and I ran into Liam."

"Pine Valley?" River cut in, breaking the unspoken rule to never interrupt the flow of a witness's thoughts.

"It's a residential memory center in Pine View. That's a town about twenty miles from here."

River met Adam's eyes but didn't speak again.

"Clover and I started visiting the center a couple of years ago. Bubbles asked me to bring her to see a friend there, and I agreed. I figured I might as well bring Clover." She shrugged. "We've been going a couple times a month since then. As a matter of fact, they're the ones who called to see if I could make a visit this week."

Adam's pulse jumped, every nerve in his body leaping to attention.

"Someone from Pine Valley called you?" he said, his voice sharper than he'd intended.

She frowned, stepping off the elevator and onto the third floor. "I did tell you about the call," she reminded him.

"I know. I just didn't realize it was from someone at that particular facility."

"Does it matter?"

Yes. It mattered a lot. He wasn't going to tell her that. Not yet. "Who called you?" he asked instead.

"Anna Randel. She's a nurse there." They'd reached the corridor that led to Bubbles's room. Adam could see the armed police officer standing outside her door. He expected Charlotte to hurry forward, rush to get to her friend.

Instead, she stopped short, her brow furrowed. "It's kind of funny, now that I think about it."

"What?" he asked, his heart pounding like a sledgehammer in his chest. He knew that whatever she said next was going to be it—the clue he'd sought since he'd joined the Special Crimes Unit, the one he'd spent three years pursuing, the one that would knock the doors wide-open and put him face-to-face with a killer.

"Anna and Liam have been dating for a year. Everyone at church thinks he's going to propose. They met at the center, and Bubbles is convinced they'll have their wedding there. She and Liam's grandmother have been friends since grade school. Dorothy was diagnosed with dementia a few years ago, and she moved herself into the center as soon as she found out, because she didn't want to be a burden on Liam."

"Why would she think she was going to be a burden?" he asked as River pulled out his phone and started texting the information to Wren and Honor.

"Like I said, Liam travels a lot. He's a medical sales rep, but more on the tech end of things. I think he sells medical software and sets it up at hospitals all over New England. Sometimes he's gone for a few days. Sometimes a week."

And there it was.

Just like that.

The connection they'd been looking for.

His phone buzzed, and he glanced at the screen, reading the message River had sent.

One word, but it summed things up perfectly: Bingo!

NINE

Suspecting that someone was guilty of something didn't make him a criminal. Charlotte reminded herself of that several times while she visited with Bubbles. Her elderly neighbor looked frail and tired, her skin wrinkled and sagging, her eyes dull.

She'd been through a lot, and it showed.

Charlotte wouldn't make that worse by trying to get more information out of her, but she wanted to ask dozens of questions. She really did.

She couldn't stop thinking about Liam. About his visits to the center and how sweet he always was to Dorothy. She didn't want to believe he was the Night Stalker. She wanted to pick Bubbles's brains to prove it to herself.

She wouldn't, though. Not until Bubbles was a little stronger, a little less scared.

River apparently had no such compunctions. He was sitting beside Bubbles's bed, a notepad balanced on his knees, a pen in his hand. Adam stood a few feet away, reading a document that Honor had sent to his phone. Their associate, Sam, was standing near the door, his height and width reminding her of a heavyweight fighter set to go into the ring.

He had more muscle than she'd ever seen on someone who wasn't a bodybuilder, his white shirt pulled taut across his shoulders. He must have felt her staring. He turned his head, met her eyes. Didn't smile. If she hadn't known he was an FBI agent, she'd have been convinced he was a criminal.

She nodded.

He returned the gesture, then went back to his original position, staring out the door.

"I can't tell you how much I appreciate your cooperation, ma'am." River spoke into the silent room, so much sincerity in his voice and in his eyes that Charlotte could almost believe he didn't have an agenda.

But, of course, he did.

She'd seen the look on his face and on Adam's when she'd mentioned Liam and Anna's relationship. She knew what they thought, knew what they were fishing for.

She'd told them what she could, but she wasn't going to offer speculations about him.

She certainly wasn't going to pretend that she'd always viewed Liam as serial killer material.

He was a nice guy. Seven or eight years older than her, a little geeky and introverted. Very likable. He'd do anything for anyone. He'd even helped her in calculus her senior year of high school. He'd been a substitute teacher, getting practical experience in the classroom because he'd planned to be a college professor, and he'd tutored after school.

He'd tutored a lot of kids.

That thought led to another. One she wasn't as happy with.

He might have tutored Bethany. He'd certainly been at the school at the same time. She'd have been a decade younger than him and completely off-limits, but that didn't mean he hadn't noticed her. That he hadn't spent a decade fantasizing about her.

"Stop it," she hissed, and Bubbles frowned.

"What's that, dear?"

"Nothing. Just…thinking out loud."

"About?"

"School," she answered honestly, and Bubbles nodded like she understood.

"Teaching is a tough job. Even for a college professor. You'll have a lot of decisions to make once you and Adam get back together."

"Bubbles!" She started to protest, but River touched Bubbles's hand, pulling her attention away.

"You were telling me about your friend Dorothy," he reminded her, and she nodded.

"We grew up together. I loved her like the sister I never had. When she met Dean, I told her that she shouldn't marry him. She did. He beat her every other day for so many years she just completely lost her will to live. If you ask me—and no one has—he's the reason why she has dementia."

"Did she have children?"

"Four. Two of them are in jail. One is dead. The other one took off when he turned eighteen. Showed up a few years later with his wife and son. By that time, Dean was dead. He was a firefighter. They say inhaling all those chemicals killed him. I say he died of his own spite. Dorothy was so happy when Ken and his family moved here. She let them build a little house on her land, and things should have been just fine, but, of course, Ken was cut from the same cloth as his father. He beat his wife and his kid. Eventually, he just walked away and left them." Bubbles shrugged. "Fortunately, Liam turned out just fine."

"Liam is Dorothy's grandson?" River asked as if he didn't already know.

"More like a son to her. He's bent over backward to take care of her these past few years. Gave up his dream of becoming a college professor so that he could be close."

He obviously had given up the dream.

But was that the real reason?

Charlotte didn't know, and she told herself it didn't matter. Liam worked hard. He took care of his grandmother. He treated Anna like she was a queen. When he wasn't helping with the youth group at church, he did the kinds of things most guys in town did. He hunted and fished, canoed and kayaked.

A few years ago, he'd purchased a piece of property near the lake, a property far off the beaten path and too close to state land to be useful for hunting. Old-timers at church had laughed at him. Liam had taken the ribbing in good stride. He'd even made a joke about it from the pulpit one Sunday, explaining that he'd needed to be that far away to keep the church youth from finding him.

Plenty of people at church had assumed that he'd open the property up to the kids eventually. Maybe bring them all out there for hiking or fishing.

But he never had, and eventually people had stopped talking about it.

Which had maybe been the point.

After all, a property out in the middle of no-where was exactly the kind of place a predator would take his prey.

She stood abruptly, her chair clattering against the floor.

The room went silent, four sets of eyes staring in her direction. She avoided them all as she turned and ran from the room. She made it to the stairwell, shoving open the door and sprinting down to the second-floor landing before Adam caught up.

He grabbed her arm, tugging her to a stop.

"Where do you think you're going?" he asked, his eyes blazing. She'd seen him angry before, but never like this. He was livid, his jaw tight, his chest heaving.

"I needed some air."

"Then you should have told me that." His hand was still on her arm, his grip firm but not painful.

"Why? So you could tell me that it isn't safe to go outside?"

"It isn't," he said, his eyes scanning her face, his expression softening. "What's wrong, Charlotte?"

"I told you. I needed some air."

"You didn't tell me why."

"Liam bought a cabin a few years back.

It's way out in the middle of nowhere. I think he has lake access, but it's not on the shore."

"There's no record of that on file with the county," he said.

"I can't tell you why not, but I know for sure he bought one. I think it was right after Daniel died, and I remember thinking how silly it all was."

"What was silly?" he asked, his voice gentle, his hand smoothing up her arm and settling on her shoulder.

"People worrying about what a guy like Liam was doing buying a cabin in the woods. I mean, our son was dead and our marriage was falling apart, and I couldn't have cared less about anything but that. But the world went on, and you left, and people stopped talking about the cabin just like they stopped talking about Daniel." She sighed, dropping down onto the stairs, her stomach churning. "I should have remembered sooner. Maybe if I had, Bubbles's house wouldn't have been destroyed. I don't even know how to tell her about that, Adam."

"I'll tell her. When the time is right."

"Do you think there is ever a good time for news like that?"

"No, but someone has to give it, and I will." He dropped down beside her, and she wanted to lean her head against his shoulder and cry for everything they'd lost.

"I'm sorry, Charlotte," he said, and she almost thought he'd heard her thoughts.

But, of course, he couldn't have.

"It's not your fault the Night Stalker planted explosives in her house, Adam. It's not your fault any of this happened." She stared at her shoes, the old scuffed tread on the stairs. She stared at her hand and the finger that had once worn the ring Adam had given her.

"Maybe it is. Or maybe it's not, but I'm not talking about the Night Stalker or Bubbles's house."

"Then what are you talking about?"

"I never should have left you, Charlotte. Not when you needed me so much."

The words were like salt poured in a wound that hadn't healed. They hurt more than she expected. She didn't want him to know that, though. She didn't want him to realize how easily he could wound her.

She'd told him the truth.

None of this was his fault.

None of what had happened after Daniel's death had been, either.

"You don't need to apologize," she managed to say, speaking through the sadness that was clogging her throat. "I wouldn't have wanted you to stay out of obligation. That would have been the wrong reason."

"I would have been staying because of love, and that would have been every right reason that ever existed."

She met his eyes—she couldn't help herself—and all the love was still there, hidden behind the pain and regret.

"Adam," she said. Just that, and he was leaning toward her, cupping her jaw the way he had the very first time they'd kissed.

And she was lost in the feel of his lips against hers. She was lost in the raspy slide of his hands down the column of her throat. She was lost in him, and she couldn't make herself want to be found.

She tasted like sunshine and summer rain. Like starlight and spring breezes. Mostly, though, she tasted like home. Adam knew he should pull back, end what he'd begun before he'd gone too far and crossed too many lines.

Only, the lines had been crossed the minute his lips had touched hers, and he didn't see any way back.

He didn't *want* any way back.

Her arms slipped around his waist, her body angling so that their knees touched. She felt as familiar as breathing, and his heart beat for her the way it had never beat for anyone else.

Behind them, the stairwell door opened, but even then, he didn't want to let her go.

"Good. I've found you both in one place. That will make discussing the plan for tomorrow a lot easier." Wren's voice was like a splash of cold water in the face, but he didn't jerk away and he didn't jump to his feet.

He released his hold slowly, his hands sliding away from Charlotte as she stared into his eyes.

"What was that about?" she murmured, and then she must have realized that Wren was standing on the landing above them. She glanced up, her cheeks pink. "Never mind. Don't answer that now."

"Not now, but I will eventually. When we have more time." He stood, pulling her to her feet and turning to face his boss.

She didn't look nearly as upset as he'd expected.

But then, Wren was like that. She adjusted to new situations, new information and new people easily.

"Well," she said, her dark gaze jumping from Adam to Charlotte and back again. "This is an interesting turn of events."

"I'm not going to apologize or make excuses," he said, and she frowned.

"I said it was interesting, not wrong. As long as it doesn't mess up my plans for tomorrow, I've got no problem with two people who are so deeply in love finding a way back to each other."

"We're not—" Charlotte began, but Wren held up a hand and shook her head.

"Don't say something you'll regret later. Come on. We've got some things to discuss. I'd like to do that before the sun comes up."

"What things?" Adam asked as she led the way out of the stairwell.

"Things that you're not going to like," she replied. "There's a conference room at the end of the hall that the hospital has agreed to let us use. The rest of the team is already there."

"What about Bubbles?" Charlotte asked. "Who's with her?"

"An ambulance crew and three members of the state police."

"An ambulance crew?" Adam wasn't sure what was happening, but it was going down fast.

"They're transporting her to another facility."

"What facility?" Charlotte demanded. "Who decided that?"

"Bubbles was given the option of staying here or going somewhere safer. She chose to go. Until the Night Stalker is found, her location is need-to-know."

"I'm one of her closest friends. I need to know," Charlotte argued.

"No. You don't, because you're in just as much danger as she is."

"I don't hear you giving her the option of going with Bubbles," Adam said. He didn't like the way things were shaping up. He knew how Wren worked. He knew she planned and executed things carefully. He also knew that she was willing to take risks if necessary. Her goal was and always had been getting predators off the streets. If that meant playing a little Russian roulette, she was sometimes willing to do it.

"I sent Savannah with her. The girl's story checked out, by the way. She ran away three years ago. She's been on the streets ever since. No record, though. She's kept her nose clean. There were no drugs in the shack or on her, and no weapons besides the utility knives. I could have let her go, but things are happening fast, and I don't want the Night Stalker to have any pawns that he can use to manipulate us."

"You also didn't want her to spend any more time on the street," Adam guessed.

"Also true. She has a little money now, but that won't last long. I've been thinking about her situation, and I have an idea that might help her secure a future, but first we need to tighten the rope around the Night Stalker's neck."

"You're talking as if we've already lassoed him."

"He lassoed himself. We're just going to pull him in." She pushed open a door and led them into a large room. Sam, Honor and River were all there, sitting around a long table that stretched nearly the length of the room. All three looked up as they entered. Honor's gaze dropped immediately, though, her focus returning to a laptop that sat in front of her.

"Go ahead and take a seat," Wren suggested. "The sooner we get started, the sooner we can end."

Adam glanced around the room. There were chairs everywhere—around the table, tucked into corners, stacked one on top of each other.

"Looks like they were expecting a big crowd," he said, pulling out a chair so that Charlotte could take a seat.

She did so tentatively, as if fear were making her muscles tense and her movements stiff.

"Don't worry," he said, leaning in close and whispering in her ear. "None of them bite."

"I'm not worried about them. I'm worried about the Night Stalker," she replied. "And Bubbles, and Savannah."

"And yourself?"

"I'm sitting in a room filled with people who are committed to keeping me safe. So, no. I'm not worried about myself."

"I'm glad to hear that," Wren said, taking a seat at the head of the table and pulling a laptop from a bag that was sitting beside the chair. "Because what I have in mind isn't for the faint of heart."

"No," Adam said, and she frowned.

"I haven't even outlined the plan."

"You don't need to. I know how you work. I know how you think, and I know exactly what you're going to suggest."

"That was a little dramatic," Honor said, typing something into the computer that sat in front of her. "I'm writing it verbatim, so that we can laugh about it later."

"Dramatic, but possible," River commented, reaching for a cup and pouring coffee into it. "He is a profiler. He's probably got us all pegged."

"Then maybe he should make this presentation," Wren suggested mildly. "Because the plan *will* be outlined and presented, and Charlotte will have a choice about whether or not she participates."

Just those words were enough to make his blood run cold.

"You're not using her as bait," he said.

"Who said that's what I planned?"

"Isn't it?"

"No. It's not." She tugged a ream of paper from the bag and passed stapled sections to everyone.

Including Charlotte.

Adam glanced at his copy, eyeing the photos of two men that were plastered across it.

"These gentlemen," Wren said, holding up the page, "are our primary suspects. Mackey Sheridan is to the right. Liam Jeffers is to the left."

"I thought Jeffers was our guy," Sam said, studying the paper as if he were committing both images to memory.

"The evidence is pointing to him, but I don't like closing doors before I make very sure there's nothing interesting on the other side of them." Wren tapped Mackey's image. "Mackey owns the butcher shop in town. According to the local police, he's gotten into a couple verbal skirmishes with patrons. He doesn't enjoy the company of others nearly as much as he seems to enjoy the company of money. He's got a lot of that. Honor obtained a warrant and accessed his tax records for the last five years. He's a millionaire several times over."

"You make that much money selling meat in a small town?" River asked. "Because if you do, I want in."

"His money is from investments. He worked on Wall Street for a few years. Ask anyone who knows anything about him, and you'll hear that he's smart. That's about all you'll hear. Most people don't know much about what he does when he's not running his shop."

"That's a lot of information in a short amount of time. You work fast," Adam said, studying the picture of the man and comparing it to the boy he remembered. Mackey had been skinny and prone to acne, his thick glasses making his eyes look huge. The man in the picture looked well put together. No glasses. No too-big suit. He wasn't smiling, but he wasn't scowling, either. "Was this taken at the butcher shop?"

"Yes. The day he opened it. The local paper ran an article."

"You'd think he would have smiled," Honor said, still typing.

"Maybe he has bad teeth," Sam suggested, turning to the next page and skimming what was written there. "This is interesting," he said. "When did we find out Jeffers had a cabin out in the woods?"

"Are you skipping ahead, Sam?" Wren asked.

"Just trying to prepare. The clock is ticking. Tomorrow is coming, and I want the Night Stalker caught."

"We got the information from public records. He paid cash and put the title in his mother's name. She'd been dead for nearly a decade by the time he bought the property, so we're going to go ahead and assume he bought it for himself. Good find on that, Honor."

"He definitely bought and used the cabin," Charlotte cut in, staring at Liam's image, her skin whiter than the paper it was printed on.

"You were out there?" Wren glanced up from her notes.

"No, but everyone in town was talking about it. No one could understand why someone would want the property. It's too close to state land to be used for hunting and there's no lake access for fishing."

"But there's plenty of solitude. No prying eyes. No one to hear if a woman happened to scream." Honor had stopped typing and lifted the page. "He could play house with his prisoner until he got tired of her, and then he could throw her away."

"Exactly," Wren agreed. "So, of the two suspects, we all agree that Liam is the one we should take a closer look at."

"How close of a look?" Adam asked, because he had a feeling they were about to get to the part of the plan he wasn't going to like.

"I think today would be a great day for Charlotte and Clover to visit the center," Wren said cheerfully as if she were announcing a field trip to the local zoo.

He wanted to tell her that it wasn't going to happen, but he kept his mouth shut and listened.

"I'm sure that Liam's girlfriend would be happy to make the arrangements. His grandmother is the one who's been requesting the therapy dog come visit again."

"How do you know that?" Charlotte asked, and Wren smiled.

"I had Bubbles call Anna to let her know that she wouldn't be able to visit Dorothy for a while. One thing led to another, and the subject of therapy work came up."

"I'm assuming you were the one thing that led to another?" River said dryly, and she grinned.

"You're assuming right. I asked Sam to

coach Bubbles, and it worked out well. Anna said that Liam has been worried about his grandmother. He's also reminded her many times of how happy Dorothy was when the therapy dog visited."

"He manipulated Anna to try to get to me," Charlotte said, and Wren nodded.

"That's how it seems. Since he's so eager to get you to the center, I think we should give him what he wants."

"I disagree." Adam finally spoke. He'd heard her out. He understood her point, but there were other ways to accomplish the goal.

"Do you have a better plan?"

"We get a warrant for his arrest, and we bring him in for questioning. While he's being interviewed, we get a warrant to search his cabin."

"That was my original plan. It's easier and has a lot less inherent risk. There's only one problem," Wren said. "He's already disappeared."

"What!" Charlotte looked stricken, her face pale.

"We were rushing to get a federal warrant issued. I think he got wind of it. Either that, or he's just worried we're onto him. A state police officer has been sitting outside his house for twelve hours, and he hasn't returned home."

"That is not what I wanted to hear," Charlotte murmured.

"Don't get too panicked yet," Honor responded. "We've established that he travels a lot."

"If he's traveling, his girlfriend isn't aware of it." Wren tapped a pen against her pages. "I called her directly and asked. She said she hadn't seen him since yesterday."

"He's slipped the net," Sam muttered.

"I don't think so," Wren replied. "He's gone to ground, but he's staying close. I checked Bethany's list of possible suspects, and he was at the top."

"Did you ask her why?" Adam asked.

"Usually I'm pretty good at doing my job," she said drily. "According to Bethany, he substituted in her calculus class during her junior year. He offered free tutoring to anyone who thought they needed help, so she went, but she felt uncomfortable from the very beginning. He stood too close when he was helping. Gave her a few too many compliments. In her words, he was creepy. She went a few times and then stopped going."

"That was quite a few years ago," Sam

pointed out. "She still has issues with him about it?"

"Not at all. She said that if that had been all that had happened, she'd have chalked her feelings up to being a teenager. After all, Liam is well respected in the community. He's a youth pastor. People like him."

"She doesn't," Adam said.

"No. She doesn't. She says he shows up at the grocery store when she's shopping, comes into the hospital while she's working and makes a point of saying hello. One night, she left work, and her tire was flat. She called her fiancé and was on the phone with him when Liam appeared. Out of nowhere was how she said it. Fortunately, she was in the car when he approached. She didn't open the door or roll down the window. She just told him she was fine and went back to her conversation."

"That must not have sat well with him," River commented.

"I doubt the engagement did, either. And now, of course, we've removed his obsession. We've made him turn his attention to something else." She glanced at Charlotte, and Adam's blood ran cold.

"What do you need me to do?" Charlotte asked.

"I'm glad you asked. Look at page three

of the packet. I've got everything outlined for you."

Charlotte did as she suggested, flipping to the page and reading it silently.

Adam did the same.

He didn't enjoy the experience, and he didn't want Charlotte to have any part of the plan that Wren had outlined. He hoped she'd feel the same. He prayed she would. He wanted justice handed to the Night Stalker the same way he wanted to take his next breath. Desperately.

But he wanted Charlotte's safety more.

That was the truth, and he wasn't going to deny it. He also wasn't going to sit and listen while Wren talked her into doing something that could cost her her life.

He eyed the third page of the document one more time, then flipped to the fourth, pulling a pen from his jacket pocket and scribbling notes for a plan that didn't include Charlotte allowing herself to be bait for a killer.

TEN

Charlotte read the plan through twice. She listened to Adam argue a case for her going into witness protection while the FBI tracked down the Night Stalker. She listened while Wren explained why that wasn't a good idea.

Even without listening, she would have known the facts.

If Liam escaped, she'd never feel safe. Even if she *were* safe, she'd always know that he was out there, hunting other victims, looking for opportunities to kill again.

She couldn't stomach the thought of that.

She knew what it was like to lose a loved one. She knew how deep the grief was, how easy it was to be consumed by it. She didn't want anyone to experience that because she'd been too afraid to do her part to stop a killer.

The choice she'd been presented with had been no choice at all. It had been a challenge. One she'd accepted.

Once she had, Wren had been all business. She'd supervised the phone call that Charlotte made to Anna. She'd put together a timeline and drilled Charlotte on what she could and could not do while she was at the center.

No walks outside.

No entering rooms alone.

She had to stay with Adam and River at all times. If, for some reason, they disappeared, she was to stay in a public area, chatting with residents until one of them returned for her.

Sam, Wren and Honor would be outside the building, waiting for Liam to arrive. Sam had left the hospital and gone straight to the center. On the off chance that Liam arrived early, they wanted to know about it. Wren had seemed confident that he would show up eventually. When he did, he'd be stalked the same way he'd stalked his victims, followed as he attempted to kidnap Charlotte.

The goal wasn't to trick him into getting her into his vehicle. The goal was to catch him with some of the tools of his trade. He'd used chloroform on all his victims. Rags soaked in the chemical had been found in four out of nine victims' cars. As a medical supply salesman, he'd probably found an easy and anonymous way to access it. He'd also apparently made himself very familiar with how long it took for chloroform to knock out its victims without killing them.

He'd made a mistake with Bethany, but he'd been rushing.

His other victims had been taken with an efficiency and ease that terrified Charlotte.

Who was she kidding?

The entire situation scared her. She didn't want to walk into the lion's den and trust God to keep her from harm. She wanted to huddle in her room and let the FBI find another way to bring the Night Stalker in.

She'd been pacing her bedroom for an hour thinking about that, praying for insight or intervention. Some miraculous occurrence that caused Liam to be arrested before she arrived at the center would be nice. Barring that, a mild heart attack wouldn't be a bad thing. At least she'd have an excuse to back out.

She glanced at the clock on her bedside table, her pulse jumping when she realized how soon they'd be leaving. Twenty minutes, and she hadn't even begun to get ready.

She dressed quickly, pulling on long yoga pants and a loose long-sleeved T-shirt that could easily hide a wire. Wren planned to have her wear one. Just in case. Unlike a traditional wired microphone, the one Charlotte would be wearing would collect audio and transmit locational signals.

It was a mini-GPS on a string.

That was what Wren had said when she'd explained it.

Charlotte was certain that was supposed to make her feel better.

It didn't.

She knew what the Night Stalker was capable of. She was walking into his territory. She was doing it unarmed, and she was trusting a team of people that she'd known for less than two weeks to keep her safe.

"What could possibly go wrong?" she muttered, grabbing Clover's therapy vest from her closet.

He pranced over, excited to be going to work.

Thanks to her gunshot and hospital stay, it had been too long since they'd gone on any visits. She wanted to be happy that they were finally getting a chance, but all she felt was dread.

"It's going to be okay," she said, strapping Clover into his vest and attaching a bow tie to his collar.

He grinned, his tongue lolling out of his mouth, his eyes sparkling.

Daniel would have loved him.

It was a thought she had several times every week. One that she had had daily when she'd first gotten the puppy. Daniel had had trouble connecting with people, but he'd loved animals. Cats, birds, horses. Dogs. Especially dogs.

"You would have been his Christmas present," she whispered to Clover, and he licked her face.

She straightened and lifted the photo from her dresser. She touched Daniel's face, reminded herself that she'd see him again one day. Knowing that had gotten her through a lot of dark and difficult days. She didn't cling to the thought as much as she used to, but it still brought her comfort.

Someone knocked on the door, and it swung open before she could respond.

She wasn't surprised to see Adam. She was surprised at how her heart seemed to reach for him, how her body yearned to move closer. She was surprised at how easily she remembered the feel of his lips against hers, the gentleness of his hands on her face. One kiss, and it had felt like everything she'd ever wished for. Everything she'd longed for in those lonely days after he'd left.

She set the picture down, her hands shaking with the force of her emotions.

"You kept this," he said, crossing the room and picking it up. "He was such a cute kid."

"He looked like you," she responded, and he met her eyes, his expression somber.

"I don't want you to do this, Charlotte," he said.

She didn't ask what he meant.

She knew.

"I have to."

"No. You don't. We can find another way to bring him in."

"What if you don't? What if he goes free? What if he disappears from the area, shows up somewhere else and starts his killing spree again?"

"Then we'll track him there, and we'll try again," he said, his tone sharp.

"And maybe you'll be successful, but not before someone else dies."

"That's not your responsibility. You don't have to sacrifice yourself to save someone else."

"I'd have done it for Daniel," she said, surprised when the words emerged, when her voice broke saying them.

"He was our son. Either one of us would have given our lives for him," Adam responded, his eyes flashing, his tone hard. "But he's gone. You're not saving him by putting your life at risk."

"You're not getting my point," she replied, angry that they were having this conversation, that she had to justify and explain herself when all she really wanted to do was walk away and forget she'd ever heard Bethany scream.

She couldn't because right was right. And doing the right thing didn't include walking away and hoping that her actions didn't cause the death of someone else.

"Then how about you tell me what it is? Make it clear, Charlotte, because I'm not accepting silence this time around."

"What's that supposed to mean?"

"Exactly what I said. After Daniel died, we buried our relationship in a mountain of unspoken words. I think we're both mature enough to speak our truths now. If we aren't, we have no business sitting in stairwells sharing our hearts."

"Sharing kisses, you mean," she said and regretted it immediately. What they'd shared had been too beautiful to be dismissed so easily as a physical thing. It had been a connection to the past, a bridge to the future. It had been a reminder of all they'd been and a glimpse of what they could be.

And she'd dragged it down to a base level, to a thing that could be as easily dismissed as a snowflake on a mountaintop.

"Is that your truth? Is it what you really believe?" he asked, setting the photo down, his eyes blazing. "Because if it is, you're more of a coward than I thought."

"I'm not the one who walked out when things got tough," she said, stung by the accusation.

"I'm going to say this one more time, and then I'm walking away." He bit the words out. "I don't want you to do this. Since you're going to, Wren will be here in five minutes to run the wire. She, Honor, Sam, River and I will be wearing earpieces. We'll be able to hear your conversations. If anything goes wrong, and you need help, all you need to do is ask."

He turned and walked away.

Just like he had before.

She could have stopped him, but she was frozen in place, afraid to call him back and afraid to let him go.

He'd been right.

She was a coward.

And she was losing a second chance at love because of it.

Pine Valley Residential and Memory Care Center was nestled in the shadow of the mountains, its redbrick facade and white picket fence designed to feel homey and inviting.

Adam would have appreciated that more if the building hadn't been so big. A four-story-high H-shaped manor house, it eclipsed several small outbuildings that stood on the property.

A place as big as the center would be easy to get lost in.

Or to lose someone in.

He frowned, glancing at his phone and the map he'd pulled up. A small dot pulsed in the center of it. The signal on Charlotte's wire was working. If something happened, if somehow Liam got to her, they'd be able to find her.

Hopefully in time.

He frowned, shoving his hand into his pocket to keep from tapping his fingers against his thigh. His nervous energy wasn't doing anyone any good. It sure wasn't making the trip any easier.

Something bumped his ear, and he turned his head, found himself looking into Clover's dark brown eyes.

"Hello," he said, and he was certain the dog smiled.

"We should have put a wire on him," Charlotte muttered to no one in particular. She certainly wasn't speaking to Adam. She'd barely looked at him since he'd walked out of her room.

He'd looked at her.

He'd seen the tension in her face, the fear in her eyes. He knew she was terrified, but the silence was there again, consuming them both.

He could let it or he could fight it.

If he did the first, he'd lose her again for sure.

If he did the second, he risked hurting and being hurt. He risked offering something and having it rebuffed. He risked his heart, but he thought that he'd rather risk it than bury it again.

River pulled into the nearly full parking lot and squeezed into a space between an old Pontiac and a shiny Toyota.

"Looks like they have a full house today," River said, opening his door and getting out.

Charlotte did the same, calling for Clover to heel, and nearly jumping from the vehicle in her rush to be away from Adam.

He let her go.

They were safe enough here. Out in the open, surrounded by people who were entering and exiting vehicles, Charlotte was a less easy target than she'd be once they entered the building. Inside, walls and doors and side entrances and exits would make it much less difficult for someone to grab her.

Someone?

The Night Stalker.

Just the thought of it filled Adam with fear and rage.

He climbed out of the Cadillac and opened the trunk, rifling through the equipment Wren kept there. He found what he wanted at the bottom of a duffel bag—a tiny wireless tracking device that could be used to follow someone or to find them. He checked the device and the tracker, making sure both were functional before he shoved them in his coat pocket and headed across the parking lot.

River, Charlotte and Clover had already reached the front door—a massive structure that seemed made for giants rather than normal-size human beings. The place was ostentatious. That was for sure. It was made for people with money, the glossy marble foyer screaming elegance and wealth. Adam walked through it, following a few steps behind the rest of the group.

According to Sam, Liam hadn't made an appearance. At least, not while he'd been patrolling the area.

Adam didn't doubt Sam's account, but he also wasn't willing to underestimate Liam's

cunning. The Night Stalker had been prac-
ticing his game for a long time. He hadn't
stayed a step ahead of the law by taking foolish chances. He'd strike when he thought no
one was looking. He'd step out of shadows no
one had noticed. He'd move quickly and with
confidence, and if the team wasn't on the top
of its game, he'd have Charlotte in his car before anyone even realized she was gone.

He frowned, stepping up beside Charlotte
as she checked in at the reception desk.

Clover sat beside her, his tail thumping
rhythmically, that comical smile on his face.

"Hey, boy. Ready for some fun?" Adam
said, crouching in front of him and pulling the
tiny tracking device from his pocket. One side
of it was strongly magnetic, and he attached it
to the underside of the dog's metal name tag as
he scratched Clover under the chin. It would
stay put until someone removed it.

"All right," Charlotte said. "We're all set.
You have to wear these while you're in the
building."

She held out lanyards with visitor badges attached, still avoiding Adam's eyes as he took
one and pulled it over his head.

"You can't avoid looking at me forever," he
said as she put on her badge and started walking toward a bank of elevators on the far wall.

"I won't need to," she responded. "I just have to keep it up until we're done here and you go back to Boston."

River laughed.

Adam wasn't amused.

"Who said I planned to go back?"

"You have a job there, a home and a life. You've got nothing here."

"Except you," he responded.

She blushed, jabbing at the elevator button and still avoiding his eyes. "We're going to the fourth floor. East Wing. The Alzheimer's and dementia unit is there. Liam's grandmother is in room 410. Should we stop there first?"

"Is that what you normally do?" Adam asked.

She shook her head. "We usually go to the activities room first. Clover loves to play fetch with the residents."

"Let's do that, then. Stick to the routine. Just in case he's watching."

She finally looked at him, her eyes wide with surprise and fear. "Do you think he's here?" she whispered.

"Sam didn't see him or his vehicle when he arrived. He asked the receptionist if Liam had been in. She said he hadn't."

"There are lots of ways into the building," River pointed out as they stepped off the elevator. "The side doors might be locked from the outside, but they're easy enough to unlock if you're inside. Do we know if Liam's girlfriend is working today?"

"She is," Charlotte confirmed. "She told me she'd be working on the first floor today. Those are the rehab patients. Usually short-term."

"The first floor would be really convenient if her boyfriend happened to want her to let him in a side door."

"That doesn't make me feel safer," Charlotte murmured as she led the way down the hall. Dark hardwood floor gleamed in the bright corridor light and several card tables and chairs were set up against the cream-colored walls. Paintings hung in neat rows, the frames the same rich dark wood as the floor. Some of them were oil paintings, professional and brightly colored. Others were drawings or chalk sketches, watercolors or collages. Adam guessed that they'd been done by the residents.

"The activities room is right around this corner. We usually spend a half hour there." She walked through a double-wide doorway.

Adam followed, his gaze skimming over the residents as he made a note of each entrance and exit point to the room. There were three. The main entrance and two doors on the adjacent walls. "Where do those doors go?" he asked as Charlotte released Clover from his leash and pulled a lightweight ball from her purse.

"One goes to a snack room. There's a fridge, stove, sink. I think the idea was to allow residents to make snacks for themselves, but as many times as I've been here, the door has never been unlocked. I only know what's in there because Anna brought me there one day."

"How about the other door?" he asked.

"Stairs. No one ever uses them. The main staircase is easier for residents to navigate, but I guess they have to be there to meet the fire escape code."

"Have you been in the stairwell?" he asked, and she shook her head.

"I never had any reason to be. I know we're here on a mission," she added. "But I can't ignore the residents. They love our visits."

She walked away, her slim body hidden beneath her heavy wool coat, the ball still in her hand.

Clover walked beside her, happy but calm.

As Adam watched, Charlotte patted an elderly woman's shoulder, said something he couldn't hear and handed her the ball. She grinned, tossing it with just enough strength to send it rolling off her lap and onto the floor.

Clover chased after it, and several people laughed.

"It's a good thing she's doing here," River said, his eyes tracking the movement of the ball as Clover carried it from one person to another, gently setting it on a lap or in a hand, and then waited patiently for it to be thrown or dropped.

"I don't just mean bringing her dog to visit people others might forget. I mean helping us bring the Night Stalker in."

"Will you be saying that if she's hurt doing it?"

"She won't be," River responded, glancing at his phone. "A moving truck just drove around to the back of the building. Sam says he's keeping an eye on it."

"Can he see the driver?"

"Negative." He frowned. "The license plate is unreadable. He can't call it in."

"I don't like the sound of that."

"Me neither. I'll go down and check it out." He jogged from the room, and Adam told himself there was nothing to worry about. People moved in and out of places like this all the time. A moving truck was a natural thing to see here, and it had rained the previous night.

Dirt and mud had probably splattered up from the road and covered the plate.

He told himself that, but he felt uneasy, his senses on high alert. He scanned the room, eyeing the residents and Charlotte. She didn't seem to think anything was out of the ordinary. But then, she was caught up playing with Clover, bringing him from one person to another with the ball.

A high-pitched screech filled the air. Mechanical and so loud that it blocked every other sound. Adam knew that some of the residents were crying and some were screaming, but all he could hear was the siren.

Charlotte ran toward him, skidding to a stop a few inches away. "Fire alarm," she mouthed. "The staff and nurses should be here shortly."

As if on cue, a dozen people raced into the room. Seconds later, it was empty. All the residents and staff gone.

The siren was still blaring.

Charlotte hooked Clover to his leash and darted away.

Adam grabbed her hand, pulling her in the opposite direction. This was the kind of situation that caused chaos. Chaos and crowds were never a good combination.

When someone like the Night Stalker was around, they were even worse.

"What are you doing?" she shouted. "We need to get out of here."

"Avoiding the crowd," he said, opening the stairwell door and tugging her inside.

ELEVEN

The siren stopped as they hit the third-floor landing, the sudden silence dizzying. Charlotte would have stopped, too, but Adam was pulling her along, his hand wrapped around hers as he sprinted down the next flight of stairs. He was on a mission, and Charlotte was part of it. Whether she wanted to be or not.

"I think maybe we can slow down," she panted, her legs shaky with the last vestiges of fear.

"Not until we're out of here."

"I might be dead from overexertion before then," she replied.

He slowed.

Not much, but enough that she didn't feel like she had to fly to keep up.

"You do know the sirens are off, right?" she managed to say through panting breaths. "The building isn't burning down."

"And the person who set them off in the first

place is probably still around? Yeah. I know. That's why I'm in a hurry." They reached the second-floor landing, still moving so quickly she couldn't catch her breath.

"You're assuming that someone did. Maybe it was a drill. Or maybe they burned the meat loaf in the kitchen. There's no reason to believe that the alarm was tripped purposely."

The door below them flew open, crashing against the wall with so much force the stairs seemed to shake with it.

Charlotte stumbled, Adam's hand tightening on hers, and then they were running again, this time up the stairs. Clover's paws tapped the concrete as they sprinted back the way they'd come.

Adam reached the door a step ahead of her, threw it open and shoved her back into the activities room.

"Do not leave this room," he said, slamming the door before she could respond.

And suddenly she was standing in the middle of an empty room, Clover beside her, the building too quiet and too still. She should have heard the residents returning by now. Voices carrying through the hall. Wheels rolling across the floor. All she heard was the thundering beat of her own heart.

She backed away from the stairwell, her gaze never leaving the door.

That was her fatal mistake, her irredeemable error.

Clover stiffened. She felt it more than saw it, his tension feeding into her, his body vibrating with a new kind of energy. He swung around, barking frantically.

She'd have turned, too, but the barrel of a gun pressed into the space between her shoulder blades.

She froze, her heart pounding so hard she was certain her entire body was vibrating with the force of it.

"Tell him to quiet down," someone said, the voice feminine and so surprising that Charlotte jumped.

"I mean it," the woman continued when Charlotte didn't respond immediately, her voice familiar and unexpected.

"Anna?" Charlotte said.

"I don't want to hurt Clover, Charlotte, but if you don't tell him to stop, I'll shoot him dead right now." She didn't confirm or deny her identity.

She didn't need to.

Charlotte was certain that Anna was behind the gun.

And that Liam was behind her actions.

"Clover. Cease," she commanded, and he fell silent except for the low rumble of a growl coming from somewhere in the back of his throat.

"Let's go," Anna said, nudging the gun so deep into Charlotte's flesh she could almost feel the cold metal of the barrel through her coat and T-shirt.

She dropped Clover's leash, took her first step with her right rather than her left foot. It was his signal to stay, something instilled in him in their first days of training heel together.

She hoped he'd obey.

She didn't want him hurt.

She didn't want to be hurt, either, and she shuffled her feet a little, moving as slowly as she dared.

"Don't," Anna said, nudging her toward the snack room.

They reached it in seconds, and the gun shifted just a little as Anna fumbled for keys to open the door.

Go! a voice in Charlotte's head screamed, and she swung around, slamming her hand against the side of the barrel.

She felt the first shot reverberate through metal and into her hand, the barrel shaking as the bullet exploded from it. The second bullet whistled past her ear as she took off, running toward the corridor, Anna screaming something behind her.

This wasn't how things were supposed to play out.

She wasn't supposed to even be navigating this alone.

She'd had the rules of engagement drilled into her head.

She knew she should be with Adam or River or both, that if she couldn't find them, she needed to seek public spaces, but the hallway was empty, the faint sound of voices drifting up from below.

She ran to the main staircase, was halfway down the first flight, when Clover yipped in pain.

She swung around, nearly falling in her haste.

Anna was at the top of the steps, one hand on Clover's collar, the other holding the gun.

"I really don't want to hurt him," she repeated.

"You already did," Charlotte responded, frozen in place, her gaze on Clover. He looked scared, his tail low and stiff, that deep growl still issuing from his throat. "It's okay, buddy," she crooned, and he offered a slow sweep of his tail.

"I didn't hurt him. I gave him a love tap. Just to let him know who's in charge. Come up here, and I'll let him go when you get back to the top."

It was a lie, and they both knew it, but Charlotte did as she was told anyway. She couldn't bear to see Clover hurt again. She couldn't stand the thought of him being mistreated by someone he'd trusted.

And he had trusted Anna.

So had Charlotte.

Even Adam's team had seemed convinced that she wasn't involved in Liam's crimes.

"This way." Anna released Clover's collar and grabbed Charlotte's arm, pressing the barrel of the gun into her side. "And don't drag your feet. The residents are on their way back up. I don't want any of them being traumatized by this."

"That's really good of you, Anna," Charlotte said, giving Clover the hand signal to stay. Adam and River had to be close. There was no way they'd left her to do this on her own.

She hoped.

Because she wasn't prepared. She had no experience with weapons or hand-to-hand combat. Even when she'd been a rebellious kid with an attitude, she'd never gotten into a fistfight.

"I didn't take you for a sarcastic person," Anna said, fumbling with the keys as they walked back into the activities room. She seemed determined to get Charlotte into the snack room.

Charlotte was just as determined to stay out of it.

"I didn't take you for a murderer," she replied. "But here we are."

"I'm not a murderer, and this isn't my fault. I'm not saying it's yours, either. We're both just doing what we think is right."

"Right? How is holding a gun on someone right?" Charlotte asked, glancing at the stairwell door. Adam hadn't appeared, and she hadn't heard a sound from beyond the door since he'd thrust her across the threshold and closed it.

Was he okay?

Had Liam somehow managed to disarm him? Hurt him?

Please, Lord, she prayed silently. *Keep him safe.*

She didn't want him to be injured protecting her.

She didn't want to lose him, either.

Not after she'd finally found him again.

Her throat tightened on the thought, her mind acknowledging what her heart had known the moment she'd opened her eyes in the hospital and seen him there.

She'd never stopped thinking about Adam.

She'd never stopped wishing he'd come back to her.

She should have told him that when she'd had the chance. Instead of pushing him away when he'd tried to get her to talk to him, she should have spoken the truth.

We're both mature enough to speak our truths now.

If we aren't, we've got no business sharing our hearts in stairwells.

The truth was, she loved him, and if she had another chance to say it, she would.

"I'm protecting someone I love from false accusations," Anna said, finally finding the correct key and opening the door.

"How do you know they're false?" Charlotte asked, her skin crawling as she stared into the dark snack room. She hadn't realized how small it was, or how black the corners of it were when the lights were off.

"Liam is the kindest, most loving person I've ever met. He won't even swat a mosquito. There's no way he could kill a human being." She jabbed the gun into Charlotte's side. "Let's go."

"Where?" She stepped into the darkness, cold dank air sweeping around her feet as Anna stepped in behind her and shut the door.

There was an exterior door opened somewhere. Or a window.

"Liam has a cabin in the woods. I've never been, but he says it's heated. Plenty of food and water. You'll be fine there."

"Neither of us will be fine if he gets us out there. I hope you know that, Anna," she said, her voice shaking. She hoped the wire she was carrying was picking up enough of the conversation to get the team moving in her direction. She hoped that someone was on the way to the rescue. She hoped a lot of things, but mostly she hoped she never, ever saw the place where nine women had been taken to die.

"Like I said, Liam is the gentlest person I know. He wouldn't hurt either of us."

"You're wrong."

"Do you think I don't know my own fiancé?" Anna huffed, grabbing Charlotte's arm and dragging her across the dark room.

"Since when are you two engaged?" Charlotte responded, her eyes finally adjusting to the darkness.

"Since last night. He told me he had to

leave town. He explained what the FBI was accusing him of, and he begged me to come with him. But, of course, he didn't want me to come without a ring on my finger."

"Wouldn't it have made more sense for the two of you to leave town right then? You have a car. No one was watching your place. Why not just go?" she asked, and the gun barrel dropped a quarter of an inch.

Obviously, Anna had been wondering the same thing.

"I suggested that, but Liam explained that we needed a distraction. Some way of throwing the federal officers off our trail."

"Come on, Anna. You're smarter than that."

"No," a man said. "She really isn't."

Charlotte tried to scream, but a hand slammed over her mouth, and she was dragged backward, the cold air she'd been feeling sweeping across her face as she was forced through a narrow opening in the paneled wall.

"Liam!" Anna cried. "Why would you say such a thing?"

"Shut up, close the panel and pull down the ladder!" he responded. "We don't have time for drama. I barely made it in here. That FBI agent nearly caught me in the stairwell, and he's probably searching every room on this floor, trying to figure out where I've gone."

The FBI agent had to be Adam, and Charlotte was so relieved to know he was alive and okay that her knees went weak.

"None of that," Liam growled, jerking her up against his side, his fingers digging into her upper arm with so much force it felt like he was trying to push them through the bone.

She felt sick with the pain, but she tried to push it out of her mind, tried to focus on the small space they were standing in. It wasn't really a room. It looked more like a pantry—shelves lining the walls, food stored in neat rows. Cans. Crackers. Cookies. Coffee. A single light bulb illuminated the small space, revealing a gleaming floor and dustless shelves.

Obviously, it *was* a pantry, and Anna couldn't be the only one who knew about it.

She stood a few feet away, looking confused and hurt and still convinced that the man who'd just called her stupid was the answer to all her prayers.

"I said," Liam snapped, "pull down the ladder."

Anna frowned but reached for a thick chord that hung from an access panel in the ceiling. She tugged, and it unfolded, revealing rickety stairs and sunlight.

"Let's go. Up the ladder." Liam shoved Charlotte so hard she fell, her knees cracking against the hardwood floor, something in her wrist popping.

He didn't give the pain time to register.

He had her by the back of her hair, was yanking her up, shoving her toward the stairs again.

"Liam," Anna cried, moving toward Charlotte, reaching for her, the gun dangling from her right hand. "What's gotten into you?"

"The need to survive," he replied. "And you've become a liability in that."

He yanked a gun from beneath his coat, and Charlotte moved, grabbing a large can of coffee from the closest shelf and throwing it at his face.

It hit its mark, smacking into his nose and cheek.

The gun jerked to the side as he fired, the bullet slamming into a bag of sugar. It exploded, white powder flying into the air. Anna screamed and screamed and screamed, her gun on the floor, her eyes wide.

There wasn't time to comfort her, to try to grab the gun or to flee.

Liam was coming at Charlotte, the gun raised, his gaze hot with anger.

"I will kill you for that," he muttered, his hand suddenly on her throat, the gun pressed into her temple.

She didn't realize what was happening until it was too late. Her oxygen was cut off, her trachea crushed beneath the pressure of his hand.

She gagged, falling into a shelf, grabbing for a weapon. Her fingers curved around a box of crackers and she slammed it into his eye.

His hand dropped away, and she gasped for breath, shoving at him, trying to get to the ladder.

She managed to take a step, and then he was on her again, slamming the butt of the gun into her temple, the sound of Anna's screams still ringing in her ears as she fell.

She didn't feel the pain.

She didn't feel anything but the desperate need to escape. He grabbed her hair, lifted her head.

And she saw it.

The gun.

Just inches away.

She grabbed for it, her fingers brushing metal.

"I don't think so," he spat, his eyes blazing as he grabbed her arm, yanked it away.

She twisted, thrusting her palm into his jaw, Anna's screams mixing with something that sounded like a dog barking.

Clover?

She didn't have time to think about that, to

wonder if her dog was on the other side of the closed panel trying to get to her.

Liam had fallen back, the blow to his chin throwing him off balance.

She wiggled out from under him, running to the folding stairs and clamoring up, cold air sweeping across her hot cheeks as she scrambled onto the roof.

Someone snagged the back of her coat, and she screamed, arms swinging, fists flying, the sun streaming down from the clear blue sky as she landed one blow and then another.

Desperate.

Frantic.

Terrified.

Determined to escape.

Please, God, she prayed, swinging her fists again and again.

Please.

Because she wanted more time to find that thing she'd been missing since Daniel died and Adam walked away. More time to let the empty places in her heart be filled, to let the broken pieces mend and to find out if what she'd felt when Adam had kissed her was real and lasting and true.

"Calm down," Adam shouted, grabbing Charlotte's wrists and trying to keep her from landing another blow as he pulled her away from the ladder and the monster who was ascending it.

She couldn't hear him.

She was blind and deaf with panic and terror.

"Charlotte," he said more gently, pulling her close, wrapping his arms around her and holding her there.

"Calm down," he repeated, and she stilled, her body stiff, her muscles tense.

"Adam?"

"Yeah," he agreed, pressing her head to his chest because he didn't want her to see what he could—Liam emerging from the opening in the roof, his hair gleaming in the sunlight, blood streaming down the side of his face.

A gun in his hand, pointed at Charlotte and Adam.

"Here's how it's going to be," Liam said as if he really thought he were going to call the shots. "I'm going down the fire escape. You're staying here. As long as that happens. No one is going to get hurt."

"I have a better idea," Adam responded, releasing Charlotte and taking a step toward Liam. "You put the gun down, I arrest you and you make your case in front of a judge and jury."

Liam laughed. "I think I'll pass on that."

"We have a warrant to search your cabin," Adam said. Not because it mattered, but because he could see Sam, moving across the roof behind Liam. Another minute and he'd be close enough to bring him down without firing a shot.

"So?"

"Want to give me an idea of what we'll find there?"

"I think you already know. If you don't, it'll be a pleasant surprise." He smiled, his eyes empty and flat.

"You killed nine women, Liam. There's nothing pleasant about that."

"Ten," Liam corrected, shifting the gun so that it was pointing straight at Charlotte's heart. His finger tightened on the trigger, and Adam rammed his full weight into Charlotte, slamming her to the ground as the morning exploded.

TWELVE

One gunshot.

Charlotte was expecting more.

A hail of bullets, maybe.

Shrapnel raining from the sky.

A cacophony of noise and confusion.

Instead, the world had gone deathly quiet.

She lay still, trapped beneath Adam, his weight pressing her into hard cement.

He shifted, his breath fanning her cheek as he raised his head and looked into her eyes.

"Are you okay?" he asked, and she nodded.

"Fine."

He frowned, touching the side of her throat. "You have bruises."

"Bruises heal," she replied. "Where's Liam?"

"Dead," he said bluntly, standing up and pulling her to her feet. He stood in front of her, and she knew he was trying to block her view, but she could see Liam's body lying prone a few feet away. Blood seeped from beneath his torso, staining the white cement rooftop. She could smell the coppery scent of it in the air. No one lost that much blood and survived. The bullet must have hit an artery.

She turned away, relieved, sad.

Liam had taken nine innocent lives. He'd planned to take hers, but that didn't mean she wanted him dead.

"Did you kill him?" she asked, her eyes trained on the horizon—the bright blue sky and puffy white clouds that drifted there.

"No," he said gently, standing behind her, his hands cupping her shoulders, his fingers resting just above her collarbones.

"I'm glad. I'd hate for you to carry that burden with you." She leaned back, letting herself accept his comfort and his support. Allowing him to see the vulnerability she'd always been afraid to show.

"It wouldn't have been a burden," he said, his breath ruffling the hair near her temple. "As much as I'd hate taking a life, I wouldn't regret doing what was necessary. Liam's finger was on the trigger. He planned to kill you, and if I hadn't been focused on getting you out of the line of fire, I'd have pulled my firearm and taken him out."

"I'm still glad you didn't have to do it."

"Thanks." His lips brushed her nape, the gentle kiss so sweet it took her breath away.

Somewhere behind them, a woman was wailing, the sound mixing with the raucous call of a blackbird and the wild barking of a dog.

"Clover," she murmured, turning around, finding herself in Adam's arms, his hands on her waist, holding her still.

"He's fine. River has him."

"You're sure?"

"Yes."

"What about Anna? She was helping Liam. Has someone—"

"Listen," he said quietly, his hands sliding up her arms, skimming along the column of her neck, his thumbs brushing her jaw.

And suddenly she was looking into his eyes, staring into their depths, while the woman's cries filled her ears.

She didn't move from Adam's embrace.

She didn't want to.

She levered up, looking over his shoulder.

Anna was kneeling beside Liam, her face red and stained with tears. There was a gun on the ground beside her and one a few feet away. Sam was there, a hulking figure who looked more protective than sinister, his brow furrowed, a phone pressed to his ear.

"Was it Anna?" Charlotte asked. "Did she shoot him?"

"Yes," Adam responded.

"What's going to happen to her?"

"Nothing. She did what was necessary to save someone else's life. She'll be taken in for questioning, but no charges will be filed."

"Poor thing. She's never going to get over this."

"Human beings are resilient, Charlotte. She'll get over it, and she'll go on."

"Still, she killed the man she loved. That's hard."

"Even if the man she loved was a monster?"

She hesitated, wondering how she'd feel if she were in Anna's place. "Probably."

"Don't feel too sorry for her. She set you up, and if things had gone the way the Night Stalker planned, you'd be on your way to whatever death he chose for you." He took her hand, leading her away from Liam's body.

"That's true, but she had no idea what he was capable of. She believed his lies, and I can't fault her for that."

"Can you fault her for agreeing to his plan to kidnap you as a distraction? I heard what she said to you. Even if she didn't believe he was a killer, the fact that he was asking her to help abduct you should have been a red flag that sent her running."

"It should have been, but Anna wanted to be part of a couple. She wanted to feel cherished and adored and special. That's what love does. It gives us validity. It makes us feel whole. Sometimes wanting it turns us into fools."

"And sometimes it turns us into the people we should be. Sometimes it helps us become our better, wiser, stronger selves. That's what loving you did for me, Charlotte."

They'd reached an open door that led into the building, and he stopped at the threshold, his dark gray eyes filled with everything Charlotte had been longing for—love, acceptance, forgiveness.

She wanted to reach for all those things and for him.

She wanted to pull him close and hold on tight, because she knew what it was like to go without. She knew the emptiness, the grief, the regret that came with being too afraid to believe that love could last.

"It's what it still does," he continued. "I have never stopped loving you. I never will. I should have said that a long time ago. I should have let you know it in a million different ways."

"You did," she said, tears clogging her throat and spilling down her face.

He wiped them away, his palms rough with calluses, his touch as gentle as the first summer rain.

"Then I should have let you know in a million more," he murmured against her lips.

When he pulled back, she had no questions. No doubts.

This was where she belonged.

He was where she belonged.

"Honor and River are waiting in the lobby. They're going to bring you back to the cottage. One of them will take your statement when you get there. The state police might want to do the same," he said, tucking a strand of hair behind her ear, his fingers warm against her cold skin.

"Where will you be?" she asked.

"I have some things to tie up here. Then I'll come home to you," he said, taking her hand and walking into the building, leading her away from the Night Stalker, away from the fear, away from the silences that she'd spent so many years dwelling in.

"You are my home," she replied, speaking the truth into the quiet stairwell, watching his face as it registered.

"You're mine, too, Charlotte," he said.

And every dream, every hope, that she'd thought had died sprang to life again.

THIRTEEN

The rhythmic pounding of a hammer on wood drifted through the evening quiet, mixing with the sound of birds chirping and squirrels bounding through the treetops.

To Charlotte, it was a beautiful symphony, a wonderful reminder of the path God had put her on, of the future He'd planned for her.

Even in the darkest hours, even when she'd felt abandoned and alone, He'd been there, guiding her steps, moving her to this time and this place where healing could finally begin.

A truck engine roared to life, the soft whir of a cement mixer making her smile.

Even with the construction going on at Bubbles's house, the lake was peaceful, the warm spring air drifting across the water as Charlotte sat in the old swing and watched the waves lap against the shore.

The kitchen window was open, and she could hear dishes clanging as Savannah cleaned up after dinner. In the month since Liam had died, life had settled into a new routine. One filled with people, activities and hope.

Hope most of all.

"Want some help?" Charlotte called to the teen, scratching Clover's fuzzy head.

"You're asking now?" Savannah replied. "I'm nearly finished."

"Better late than never," Bubbles intoned. She'd completely recovered from her near-drowning, and she'd taken up knitting. Something to keep her hands occupied until she could return to her own home.

Her new home.

The old Victorian had been demolished.

Picking through the ashes of what remained had been difficult, but Bubbles had weathered that like she did everything. With grace, aplomb and faith. She'd planned to move to the Pine Valley Residential and Memory Care Center until her new house was built, but Charlotte had plenty of room in the cottage.

And plenty of room in her heart.

For Bubbles.

For Savannah.

For Adam.

He'd been true to his word.

He'd returned home to her, staying in the cottage with the team while the investigation into the Night Stalker was completed. Once the case was closed, he'd rented an apartment in Whisper Lake. He stayed there on the weekends and in Boston during the week. Charlotte had told him it was too much, that the commute was too hard, but he'd continued to make it.

He'd been back in her life for six weeks, and it felt like they'd never been apart. When he was in town, they spent every minute they could together. When he was away, she yearned to have him back.

"You're smiling," Bubbles said, looking up from the mustard-yellow knitting project she was working on.

"I'm happy."

"Of course you are, dear. Adam is back. Just like I knew he would be, and the two of you can start again, building the life you should have had all along."

"Maybe we'll build something different than that," Charlotte said. "Something even better."

"That, too, my dear," Bubbles responded, holding up her project and frowning. "Does this look like a sweater to you?"

It looked like a droopy misshapen map of Florida, but Charlotte didn't have the heart to tell her that.

"Well—"

"No," Savannah called from inside the house. "It does not."

"Savannah," Charlotte chided. "Sometimes silence is the better part of valor."

"And sometimes it's the same as a big fat lie." The teen walked out the back door, wiping her hands on the frilly apron she'd tied around her waist. She looked softer than she had the day they'd met, her purple hair fading, the roots coming in a deep burnished red. She still wore her combat boots and ear studs, but she'd removed the eyebrow piercings and most of the attitude.

Therapy was helping.

So was getting accepted into the community college.

Charlotte had encouraged her to do both.

She'd made Savannah's first appointment with the counselor, and she'd driven her to the community college for placement tests. She'd cheered her on as she'd applied for financial aid, gotten her college ID and her books for the two classes she was planning to take in the summer.

She'd watched as Savannah began to relax, as she'd slowly begun to feel at home. The two-thousand dollars Wren had given her had offered Savannah hope that the future would be better than the past had been. Charlotte had offered her the rest—a place to stay as long as she needed it, someone who believed in her. A voice of encouragement that would hopefully one day drown out the voices from the past.

Savannah still hadn't opened up about her life prior to running away, but she'd begun to plant herself firmly in the rich soil of acceptance that Charlotte and Bubbles were offering her.

"In this case, I prefer honesty to a lie." Bubbles studied her creation and sighed. "I'm starting to think I'm not all that good at knitting. Which is a shame. I was planning to make all of you sweaters for Christmas."

"You're not bad at it," Savannah said, sitting next to Bubbles and taking the knitting from her hands. "You just need to concentrate a little more. Watch me."

She started knitting, her stitches quick and tight and beautiful.

"Where did you learn to do that?" Charlotte asked, and she shrugged.

"I wasn't always a runaway." She glanced at the book Bubbles had taken the pattern from and continued the project, humming quietly as she worked.

"You know, Bubbles," she said, "if you really want to make sweaters as gifts, you might want to choose prettier colors."

"You don't like the color? I think it's lovely," Bubbles exclaimed.

"Lovely if you like mustard. I prefer butter yellow and golden sunsets and green-tinged moonlight on the lake. Maybe tomorrow we can go to town? I can take you to the knitting store and help you pick some really pretty stuff."

"Well, I guess I couldn't turn my nose up to that," Bubbles responded. "A date with my favorite girl will heal the pain of knowing that she despises my taste."

Savannah laughed, handing the knitting back to Bubbles. "I don't despise it. Maybe I even like it. As a matter of fact, it's possible I was just being rude because I wanted an excuse to spend more time with you."

"Sure. I'll tell myself that as I cry myself to sleep tonight." Bubbles set the knitting down. "We do need to go to town, though. I still need to pick up the flowers for…" Her voice trailed off, her face flushing.

"Bubbles," Savannah hissed. "That's a surprise."

"What kind of surprise?" Charlotte asked.

Bubbles and Savannah gave her matching looks—faked confusion, furrowed brows.

"Surprise?" Bubbles said. "Who said anything about a surprise?"

"Savannah did, and you obviously know exactly what she's talking about."

"Maybe I do." Bubbles stood, planting her hands on her narrow hips. "And maybe I'm too good at keeping secrets to spill the beans. If Adam wants to plan something like this without consulting you—"

"Bubbles," Savannah shouted, jumping to her feet. "You're going to ruin everything."

"I most certainly am not," Bubbles huffed. "And mind your tone when you're talking to me. I am your elder, after all."

"And I'm your favorite girl, remember?" Savannah retorted. "Because I keep you out of trouble and make sure you don't knit ugly sweaters for Christmas presents."

"Well!" Bubbles huffed.

"Ladies, how about we all just calm down?" Charlotte tried to intervene, but the two were on a roll, and she'd learned from a month of experience that they liked it that way.

"Calm down?" Savannah growled. "Calm down? She's going to ruin all the planning we've been doing. And I am not going to stand around here watching it happen. Come on, Clover," she snapped. "Let's go for a walk."

She stalked to the door and probably would

have walked inside, but Adam appeared in the doorway, his hair mussed, his eyes shadowed, his gaze sweeping over the little group and landing on Charlotte.

He smiled, and everything in her smiled back.

"Adam," she said, jumping to her feet. "I didn't think you'd be back in town until the morning."

"My schedule opened up, so I thought I'd come early," he said. "I knocked, but no one answered."

"You know you don't have to knock. The door is always opened to you."

Savannah snorted. "You two get cornier every time I see you," she said, but there was a touch of wistfulness in her voice and in her eyes.

"They're not corny. They're in love," Bubbles responded.

"We're also not opposed to having time alone," Charlotte said. Neither of her housemates got the hint. They stayed right where they were, looking on as she took Adam's hand and led him across the deck.

"You look tired. How about we go for a walk, and you tell me about your day?" she suggested, and he smiled, that easy gentle smile that she loved so much.

"Actually, I had other plans."

"Do they include chocolate?" Savannah asked. "Because I have a hankering for some, and the snack cupboard is currently empty."

Adam ignored her, his focus on Charlotte. Something in his eyes, in the somberness of his expression, made her pulse race.

"What's wrong, Adam?" she asked, and he shook his head, touched her cheek, letting his finger trail down to the pulse point in the hollow of her throat.

"Nothing. When I'm with you, everything is right," he responded. "I've missed you, Charlotte."

"I've missed you, too. The weeks are long without you around, but at least we get to have the weekends together." She kissed him, just a gentle touch of lips, and he smiled.

"I guess I'm not making myself clear."

"You're not," Savannah cut in. "A kindergartener could do it better."

"Hush," Bubbles chided. "He's a grown man. He can handle this without your help."

"Hopefully," Adam murmured, his gaze steady and unwavering.

"I really don't know what's going on," Charlotte said. "But it might be easier to figure out without the peanut gallery around."

"We can leave," Bubbles said, grabbing Savannah's hand.

"Stay," Adam responded, still staring into Charlotte's eyes.

"What I'm trying to say is that I miss what we had, Charlotte," he said quietly. "The late-night talks in front of the fire. I miss waking up with you beside me. I miss reaching out for you in the middle of the night and knowing you'll be there. I miss that feeling of contentment I used to get, knowing that you were in the house with me, that we shared the same space, the same world."

"We do share the same space and the same world." She pressed her hand to his chest. "We always have."

He covered her hand with his, pressing it closer. "I should never have walked away from you."

"Daniel's death was hard on both of us," she said, her voice tight, her chest aching. "We were young."

"No. We were scared. We were both too afraid to let the other know how deeply we were mourning, how dark our lives had become."

"You're right," she admitted. "I'm still afraid. I don't want to ever feel that kind of hurt again."

"I can't guarantee you won't, but I can guarantee that I'll stand beside you through whatever comes. I love you, Charlotte. Will you marry me again?" he said, and she could only nod, tears streaming down her face as he reached into his pocket and pulled out a ring set with a yellow-green stone.

"It's beautiful," she said, touching the square-cut gem.

"It's Daniel's birthstone," he said, and her breath caught, her heart aching with joy and with sorrow.

He pulled her into his arms, kissing her gently and passionately, promising without words that he'd do exactly what he'd said—stand beside her. Always and forever.

"I love you," she whispered against his lips. "And I can't wait to marry you again."

"That's good to know," he said, taking her hand and leading her across the deck. "Because we've already set the date."

"We?"

"Yeah." He gestured to Savannah and Bubbles. "We discussed it last weekend, and we decided that sooner is better."

"I agree," she said, patting Clover's head as he nudged between them.

"Great!" Savannah said, wiping something that looked suspiciously like a tear from her cheek. "I went to that little boutique in town and bought you the prettiest white dress. Lots of lace and eyelet. It's really flowy. You're going to love it."

"And I chose the shoes," Bubbles cut in.

"I returned them. You'll like my choice better, Charlotte. You have an appointment to get your nails done tomorrow, and the cake is going to be delivered to the church right after service on Sunday."

"Sunday?" Charlotte repeated, her head spinning as she tried to understand what they were saying.

"Your wedding day," Savannah said, glancing at her watch and whistling softly. "And we've got a ton to do before then. You got your suit, right, Adam?"

"Right."

"And I need to get the bow tie for Clover. The pastor is all for having him at the church. We're going to have a potluck after the ceremony. Nothing fancy, but I think it will be fun." Savannah tore off her apron and grabbed Bubbles's hand. "Now that I'm thinking about it, we should probably get the flowers now. And the bow tie. And maybe a few other things."

"We'll have time tomorrow," Bubbles said.

"Sure we will, but they want time alone

now," Savannah hissed, dragging her into the house.

"Wow," Adam breathed. "I had no idea what I was getting myself into when I asked them to help."

"The three of you planned a wedding in a week?" Charlotte said, still not certain she understood.

"We had a little help. Wren and Honor made the invitations and had them hand-delivered to everyone at your church."

"But...you planned it in a week?"

"We did, but it can be changed if you'd rather wait. We can have the wedding in a month or a year. Whenever you're ready, I will be," he said.

"I'm ready," she said, her heart leaping as he smiled.

"I was hoping you'd say that," he said, pulling her in for another kiss. "Because as far as I'm concerned, Sunday can't get here soon enough."

She laughed, taking his hand and calling to Clover.

They walked down to the beach, the moon rising above the distant mountains, the water that Charlotte had hated for so long lapping at the shore. She didn't notice the inky black-ness now, though. She didn't think about the darkness or the depth or the danger of it. She focused on the lights that twinkled on its surface, a sweet reminder that she had never been alone. God had been there through the darkest days, and He would be there through the brightest.

She squeezed Adam's hand, but she didn't speak. Her heart was too full for words.

He seemed to understand.

He pulled her closer, his arm around her waist, his steps matching hers, every part of them in sync as they turned back toward the cottage and walked into their future together.

* * * * *

Dear Reader,

Last year, my ten-year-old niece was diagnosed with a very aggressive form of sarcoma. As you can imagine, this was devastating for our family. I have watched my sister travel this very difficult road, and I have been reminded of how short life is. More than that, I have been reminded that bad things often happen to good people. None of us are exempt from heartache and none of us are immune to doubts and struggles. He is here, though. In the darkest times and in the brightest ones. If you doubt it, look at the moonlight dancing on an ocean wave, watch the goldfinches flit from branch to branch and listen for the sound of His love whispering through the leaves of the tallest oak tree. You will find Him there.

In the FBI: Special Crimes Unit series, I explore the darker side of human nature. The men and women who work for this elite team each have unique backstories and traumas that have made them determined to protect the most vulnerable citizens. Like us, they sometimes wonder if God dwells in the toughest places. I hope you'll journey with them as they find their answers and learn the truth of His extraordinary grace and love.

Blessings to you, my friend.
Shirlee McCoy

Get 2 Free Books,
Plus 2 Free Gifts—
just for trying the Reader Service!

Love Inspired®

Get 2 Free Books,
Plus 2 Free Gifts—
just for trying the
Reader Service!

HOME *on the* RANCH

YES! Please send me the **Home on the Ranch Collection** in Larger Print. This collection begins with 3 FREE books and 2 FREE gifts in the first shipment. Along with my 3 free books, I'll also get the next 4 books from the Home on the Ranch Collection, in LARGER PRINT, which I may either return and owe nothing, or keep for the low price of $5.24 U.S./ $5.89 CDN each plus $2.99 for shipping and handling per shipment*. If I decide to continue, about once a month for 8 months I will get 6 or 7 more books, but will only need to pay for 4. That means 2 or 3 books in every shipment will be FREE! If I decide to keep the entire collection, I'll have paid for only 32 books because 19 books are FREE! I understand that accepting the 3 free books and gifts places me under no obligation to buy anything. I can always return a shipment and cancel at any time. My free books and gifts are mine to keep no matter what I decide.

268 HCN 3760 468 HCN 3760

Name	(PLEASE PRINT)

Address	Apt. #

City	State/Prov.	Zip/Postal Code

Signature (if under 18, a parent or guardian must sign)

Mail to the **Reader Service:**

IN U.S.A.: P.O. Box 1867, Buffalo, NY. 14240-1867
IN CANADA: P.O. Box 609, Fort Erie, Ontario L2A 5X3